Seeing Gail Again

by

Larry Farmer

Seeing Gail Again

Cover Art by *Tina Lynn Stout*

The Wild Rose Press, Inc.
PO Box 708
Adams Basin, NY 14410-0708
Visit us at www.thewildrosepress.com

Publishing History
First Vintage Rose Edition, 2017
Print ISBN 978-1-5092-1718-2
Digital ISBN 978-1-5092-1719-9

Published in the United States of America

She stopped walking in order to hug me again, then looked up to kiss me. I had forgotten how a kiss from Gail made me feel. Special. Deep. Real. It touched me that she chose to kiss me so spontaneously. She wasn't the type to do so. It was as if the ice was breaking inside her and our former feelings were transitioning to the here and now. Somehow our past was renewing the present.

I pulled back from her long enough to take off my backpack yet again, then returned to our embrace. I wanted more of this. Right now. I wanted to make up for the lost years all in one swoop, if I only could before we reached her place.

"I've dreamed of kissing you again," she said, looking up at me from our embrace. "Like this, right here at the train station, as if we're part of an old-time movie. I was so reserved before I met you, and became so again after our separation. So I wasn't sure I could go through with it. But I wanted to renew us; I fantasized about meeting you again."

"I like this version of Gail," I said softly. "Eight years seems so long ago, with all that was between us at the Lakes. But it's becoming real again now."

Dedication

To my ol' Army partner in crime, John David Lash.
And in loving memory of
William Stone "Buddy" Hargrove

Chapter 1

The train slowed into Manchester station as I focused on the crowd of people at the dock. Would Gail look different from how I remembered her? We were in our late twenties the last time we saw each other, four years ago, back in 1977, a month after Elvis died. I knew I was a different person now. Gail had seemed different, too, in her letter inviting me to come see her.

Were we just older? Was that the difference?

It was part of it, I was sure. After all, we first met eight years before, in the summer of 1973, and not far from here, in the English Lake District near Scotland. That was a fairytale back then, I thought, reminiscing while I searched for her from the train.

As we slowed to a stop, I grabbed my backpack from the luggage rack and made my way to the exit door of the train compartment. I wanted to be the first one out. I wanted to see her waiting for me.

Suddenly there she was, waving as she made her way through the crowd at the train dock just a few feet away. Her hair was cropped, her expression sullen, a few pounds added to her still-slim figure wrapped in a brown cotton blouse with matching slacks.

She still looked so much like Dolores Hart, my favorite actress while I was growing up after I saw the movie *Where the Boys Are*. Gail's reserved demeanor, like the girl's in the movie, had melted me. It was as if she knew something but didn't know how to relate it to anyone. But the solemnity I saw now in Gail was somehow different as I approached her, watching her watch me. She seemed older inside. Tired.

"It's good to see you, Jericho," she said, reaching out to hug me. I laid my backpack down so I could embrace her. "I remember you being tall," she noted while easing into a slight smile, "but I forgot how much so. Thank God you are, though—it made it easier to find you in the crowd. How tall are you, again? Still that blond hair and blue eyes. Like me. Still wearing blue jeans after all these years. But sneakers instead of boots. And a T-shirt. Mr. Casual."

"I was so glad to get your letter," I said, then remembered she'd asked me a question. "I'm six three."

"Six three? How could I have forgotten? A full eight inches on me. And you still have muscles," she commented. "Still the Marine."

"Yeah, I was just out of the Marines and Vietnam when we first met back in the Lakes, wasn't I?"

"Come on," she said, pulling at me to walk me out of the station. She barely gave me time to put on my backpack. "We'll talk on the way. My car is parked nearby. It's a small Austin. Do you remember the old one? I was surprised you could get in that, before. I hope you can this one, also."

"You were a teacher then," I remembered out loud, "when I came here to Manchester four years ago to see you."

She nodded.

"But now I've just lost my job," she said, her expression all the more somber with that revelation. "I quit my teacher's position for one in counseling, and then was let go with budget cuts a couple of months ago. I didn't mention it in the letter because I wanted you to come. I wasn't sure you would if I told you."

"Why wouldn't I?" I asked, bewildered.

"I was so surprised that you're living in Bern now," she said, apparently needing to change the subject. "That's just down the road from England. And you've been there since the spring. It's autumn now. It seems a waste of time—the entire summer not knowing each other's whereabouts. I could have visited you. It took a fortnight, as it was, for my letter to reach your address in Texas and be forwarded to your new address in Switzerland."

She stopped walking in order to hug me again, then looked up to kiss me. I had forgotten how a kiss from Gail made me feel. Special. Deep. Real. It touched me that she chose to kiss me so spontaneously. She wasn't the type to do so. It was as if the ice was breaking inside her and our former feelings were transitioning to the here and now. Somehow our past was renewing the present.

I pulled back from her long enough to take off my backpack yet again, then returned to our embrace. I wanted more of this. Right now. I wanted to make up for the lost years all in one swoop, if I only could before we reached her place.

"I've dreamed of kissing you again," she said, looking up at me from our embrace. "Like this, right here at the train station, as if we're part of an old-time movie. I was so reserved before I met you, and became so again after our separation. So I wasn't sure I could go through with it. But I wanted to renew us; I fantasized about meeting you again."

"I like this version of Gail," I said softly. "Eight years seems so long ago, with all that was between us at the Lakes. But it's becoming real again now."

"Do you remember the song you sang me that night we camped out on the peak at Brim Fell back then, back in '73?" she asked me. "The Hank Williams one. That song describes how I felt when I saw you just now as you got off the train. I still remember the title, 'I Can't Help It If I'm Still in Love with You.' Do you remember singing those words to me, like some anthem, in our time at the Lakes? Even my memories of us from our days there weren't up to the feeling just now of seeing you again. How can I be this corny?" She gave a little laugh. "But it's true. And I knew that I would indeed kiss you dramatically at the train station now, just like I've fantasized ever since I knew from your last letter that you were coming to see me."

To remember Gail when I first met her, how proper she was in her mannerisms, and then to see her respond to me with abandonment as we fell for one another…well! Hers was the greatest seduction experience of my life. Now here, again, in public, in a train station in England, the metamorphosis took place so fluidly before my very eyes, so quickly. It was as if these feelings had never been otherwise.

"I know it sounds silly for me to fret about your reaction to my situation, living on the dole now," she said, coming back down to earth. "I'm sorry I didn't give you the benefit of the doubt that you'd come see me. But my layoff only recently happened, and I feel so vulnerable. It's another reason I didn't come see you in Bern. I didn't want you to feel I had a motive."

That explained her look when I saw her in the

crowd. Not tired so much as vulnerable. I hated her circumstances but loved her for her vulnerability.

"You're exactly the one I want to see now, Jericho," she said as she broke away from our embrace. "To make up with you, after what happened the last time we saw each other, four years ago, back in 1977 when I rejected you. Some karma going on, I think. You were so silly back then, I have to say. You seemed so lost, yet I was happy to see you again when you appeared, from out of nowhere, on my doorstep right here in Manchester. To me it was just old times with an old friend, but to you it was as if I'd betrayed you, as if I had run off with another man. You didn't like the mere fondness I showed you; you expected more of that summer in '73 at the Lakes about us, while I thought we had moved on from all that."

The memory of her rejection four years ago still stung me as she mentioned it. She reached down to pick up my backpack, with a struggle, and hand it to me.

"Let's continue on, my dear," she instructed. "We'll talk in the car."

Her car was so small I barely managed to get my backpack inside and into the back seat. With some stretching, bending, and swaying, I fitted myself into the passenger seat.

Once we were on the road, Gail reached over with her left hand to hold mine. In England, since they drive on the left side of the road, the driver and steering wheel are on the right side of the car. I loved the British for this. They were unique and special, stubbornly so.

"I'm glad you wrote me, Gail," I said to break the silence.

She glanced at me as we shared a smile.

"I need to make a turn," she said apologetically, letting go of my hand.

"I love your hands," I said, still looking straight ahead, embarrassed at how it sounded. "How soft they are."

"Whatever happened to that Israeli girl you met during the Yom Kippur War back in 1973?" she asked as she steered the car into a side street. "Back when you left me to save the day for them. I was jealous, even though I could tell you were just having a fling. All the more reason to think we were moving on with our lives after you left the Lakes. I would never have told you if I had a boyfriend. I thought this was perhaps a culture clash between us. I didn't know what to think, actually. You still wrote the most endearing letters while that relationship was going on there in Israel. You acted like she was some pet you were walking and I was supposed to understand."

"I don't know what I was thinking," I mumbled. "She was fun."

"I bet she was." Gail snickered.

"I was so in love with you," I explained, "and at the same time I was in this exotic place and setting…"

"What's exotic about a kibbutz?"

"There was a war going on, Gail. I didn't see the war itself, but I was part of it, nevertheless. And I knew if the Arabs won we'd all be wiped out. Besides, I had never been on a kibbutz before. I'd never even heard of a kibbutz. It was somewhat exotic to me because of that."

"How could a Jew not hear of a kibbutz? Even if you are from Texas and halfway around the world, this doesn't make sense."

"My thoughts exactly. Now. We didn't have many Jews down in my little two inches of rural Texas. Even in college, we didn't have a rabbi. There was a Hillel, but it was just a meeting place for students to get away and feel Jewish."

"You didn't read Jewish history?" she quizzed.

"I'm sure I came across mention of a kibbutz somewhere, but it didn't register. Jews were going to Palestine to settle at the turn of the century and during the British Mandate. Some of those Jews were socialists from Russia. I don't remember what all I read about that sort of thing. I hadn't a clue there were communal farms still going on now."

"You're the smartest man I've ever met, Jericho, so that seems unreal. For you to not know that. Anyway, it was exotic to you. I'll give you that. That part makes a bit more sense, I suppose. Exotic, and so anything goes. Is that right? Do as you will in the candy store?"

I shrugged but let my feeling of guilt show.

"I know I shouldn't have mentioned her back then," I replied. "I was so in love with you. I did feel awkward mentioning her, but I was in the middle of this huge adventure and couldn't keep myself from telling you things. Poor excuse, but that's what happened. I have time to feel stupid now."

That cheap excuse didn't satisfy me, and I was sure it didn't satisfy Gail. I sighed, looked at her as she drove, and searched for more honest explanations.

"The real reason I told you about her," I continued, "is because I thought we'd never meet again. That I'd never see you again. That you'd move on in your nice, stable life. I still didn't know what I wanted in mine. I hadn't found myself. I held on to you emotionally but

7

felt I'd better forget you. That you wouldn't be there for me very long. And maybe I should find a Jewish girl while I was in Israel and seek my identity as a Jew." I looked at Gail meekly. "I'm sorry. I ruined everything and deserved how you treated me when I looked you up here in Manchester four years later."

A smirk appeared on her face, but then she shook her head in bewilderment as she switched on the blinker and turned her car into a narrow driveway in front of a white wood-frame cottage.

"This is me flat," she explained. "It's small but divided into two—a duplex, you would say—so it's even smaller where I live in my half of it. It's all I can afford, now I'm on the dole."

She came to a stop, glanced at her wristwatch, then opened the car door to get out. I followed her into her house, dragging my backpack along.

"I could never expect better from you," she said as we walked. "I'm aware of it. You've still got your looks. What girl wouldn't want a piece of you?" She glanced at me, wearing a pathetic scowl. "I can say that now, all these years later. I loved your letters from Israel, but it comes back to me how I almost hated you for them, too."

Chapter 2

Inside her apartment, she led me past the small living room and on through the hallway into her bedroom.

"We'll sleep here, my pretty," she instructed. "Lay your rucksack against the back wall near the bathroom."

I did so, and then we left for her kitchen, which was on the other side of the living room. She left me to sit at the small dining table with its two chairs, and went immediately to boil water for tea, as well as get out a small chocolate cake from her refrigerator. After placing the cake on the table near me, she brought out two cups for our tea and two small saucers for the cake. Then, patiently, she went back to the stove to wait for the tea to boil. All the while she kept her back to me as much as possible.

"Lemon, dear?" she asked as she brought forth the teapot. She began to pour into my cup. "I forgot if you like lemon in your tea. We didn't have much tea together, did we? Americans prefer coffee, and I expanded my horizons with you about it, back in the day."

"Yes, I'll take lemon," I said with a polite smile, "and some honey, if you have any."

"That's right. You used to put honey with your cream in your coffee. The only person I've met that did such. It's charming, in a way. How could I forget such a quirk? Yes, I do have some honey, in fact. I'll get it for you. I seldom use it, but it has shelf life."

She brought out the lemon and the honey and set them in front of my cup of still-steaming tea. Busily, she cut a piece of the cake for each of us. As she sat down, she glanced at her plate with the cake, as if inspecting. She then directed her attention at me, grabbed both of my hands to hold affectionately, and stared solemnly into my eyes before speaking.

"Let's just touch a bit while the tea cools. Just to link again. Do you mind, Jericho? A touch is so precious."

Her intensity of emotion melted me. I began stroking the backs of her hands with my thumbs.

"I've been marking time since I discovered you gone," she said. "I mean really gone. I'm talking about after you huffed out of here four years ago, never to be seen again. As my life got more drab, I kept thinking of you. And noticing you gone. So gone. No one ever hurt over me like you did then, when I rejected you. No one ever did any of the things that you did about me in our relationship, in fact. And I thought, 'He's special.' It came to me just like that. Some revelation of sorts. 'He's so incredibly special.' For the past four years, now, I've kept hoping your memory would go away and either I would adjust to a bland reality or I would find Mr. Right. But nothing. Nothing but memories. Of you. Of wanting you and what you gave me. Of wanting 'special' back in my life."

A tear rolled down her cheek.

I wanted to explode emotion all over her and grab her to hold. I watched that tear make it to the corner of her mouth before finally tapering to a stop.

"The tea is ready to drink now, I'm sure," she said, letting go of my hands.

She looked down at her cup before taking a sip. Mists of steam oozed upward onto her face, and she began to blow softly to cool the still-hot tea. Then she looked back at me, staring once again straight into my eyes.

"I have stories to tell you, also," she said in a straightforward business tone. "Of men in my life. Looking for Mr. Right, as I said. I could color them up to make you jealous, and I almost feel like it again, just thinking of your Israeli-girl adventure. Some of the men I admired, or thought charming. Some were handsome. But none were you. I kept telling myself how I didn't want you. The problem was, I didn't have you. And any new man in my life after you simply bored me, to be blunt. That seemed childish to me, to be bored by men that I would have otherwise felt decent with. Because of how our deep relationship in the Lakes was so abruptly ended with your departure to Israel, I felt I couldn't take you seriously. Then the Israeli girl you were telling me about, and then your later adventuring... All of this only made me more certain it was best to simply leave you in my past, in spite of my feelings for you. I didn't at all doubt how I felt inside. But our time in the Lakes was supposed to be just a period in my life. I was sure of it. Like some romantic version of a Disney movie. With you the hero, until the fantasy is over, and he's moved on, without me, into a world where I could never belong. I thought I belonged here in England. I knew I did. Why was I longing for someone in something that was just a glorious, even if heartfelt,

11

time? The word 'fling' doesn't really fit, but I just couldn't take our relationship seriously, even if my feelings for you were real. But the truth of the matter is, you ruined it for everyone I ever met after you."

She took a sip of her tea while I continued to sit in silence, taking in the meaning of her words.

"Not fair, is it?" she asked with self-mocking. "I'm glad you told me just now about all you felt while you were in Israel with that girl. How her being Jewish mattered to you at the time, in your circumstances, that the time there was special, that you didn't know what to do with your life, so any feelings for me seemed like some inconvenience. That's a trite way to put it, but the point is, I get it. In my own way, I get it vividly. Yes, I thought I had a stable life and that I knew what I wanted. You were the opposite from me in how you didn't seem to know anything about yourself. Yet in some ways you had it better. You at least knew you didn't know what you wanted. My point is that after you, suddenly, I didn't know what I wanted anymore. I kept telling myself I did, but I found out first hand just how I didn't. It seems we reached the same conclusions about ourselves from two different directions, and it took the years to sort it all out with us."

"That's why I came to see you four years ago, right here in Manchester," I reminded her. "Because I had finally sorted it all out. I loved you. I loved you like no other in my life, before or after you. And then there you were, wondering what I was doing holding on to the past."

She turned away with a grimace, then nodded before looking back at me.

"In a way, I had gotten over you," she said. "I

thought I must, for survival. Appreciating our time together in the Lakes but thinking it was just this beautiful time in a beautiful setting but one I couldn't trust. Carried away by the moment or something. And then you were so ready to leave me for a cause, for an adventure in Israel, where you had to mention a Jewish girl that you seemed to wish was Miss Right. Then you left her too, for more adventure. To take up for myself, what was I supposed to think or do about you? Now, tell me."

I nodded sympathetically to her and felt every ounce of disgust for myself that I deserved.

"Missed opportunity." I sighed. "On both our parts."

She turned away for a moment, then back toward me, retaining her serious demeanor to give me a nod of agreement at my statement.

"Have some cake," she offered shyly, breaking the awkwardness.

"Are we going to talk first or make love?" I asked bluntly.

"Let's talk first, my dear. Once we go to bed, I don't know when we'll get up again. Let's shower first, even then. I want to be fragrant for you before I sweat all over you."

She winked at me before sipping her tea.

"How on earth did you wind up in Switzerland?" she asked, changing the subject. "Come, eat up. The cake is marvelous. It's a chocolate cream cake. We have the greatest bakery down the street. I thought of you and bought this. I know you love chocolate so much. Switzerland's a grand place for the likes of you, is it not? All that chocolate. Toblerone, Lindt, and who knows what other manufacturer of ambrosia they must have there. I envy you."

I began my explanation to her question about my living now in Switzerland. "You may remember when we were waiters at our luxury hotel restaurant in Bowness, how everybody loved the cowboy waiter from Texas?"

"My word, yes!" She swooned at the memory. "It was sickening. Everyone wanted to be waited on by you. This tall cowboy right out of a John Wayne movie, Texas drawl and everything. All the tips you got, even if you spilled food all over them. You were the worst waiter in history, but people fawned over you, masochists that they were."

"Well, I got more than tips because of all that."

"You did not, I repeat, not, as in did not, have affairs with any of those bimbos, my sweet, because I am living proof you spent every spare moment with me on our after hours."

"That's true, Gail. But it doesn't mean I didn't get a million addresses. Australia, Kenya, South Africa, Japan, Denmark, Germany..." I paused for effect. "Switzerland."

"Wait a minute. Don't bottle up my juices before they start flowing. Is there going to be a story behind one of those Swiss addresses that's going to ruin our lovemaking that just might not take place if you piss me the hell off right now?"

"No, no, no. Wait a minute. My Swiss address was of a family in Zurich. But they were real nice people, and Jews. Everyone wants to see Switzerland, so I made sure to save that address. But then later on, when I was in Israel, two doors down from me was a Swiss nurse. From Bern. Blonde-haired, with incredibly abundant mammary glands."

"Big boobs were they, now? We're still at jeopardy about our post-tea endeavors, Jericho. You'd better lie to me if you have to. How did a gorgeous blonde nurse from Bern, Switzerland, with big boobs, not be a major factor in Israel, at this exotic kibbutz? Your lie better convince me, or you're sleeping on the couch."

"It's a perfect excuse, Gail. I don't even have to make it up."

I heard her foot tapping impatiently on the floor.

"So, back to the scene at the hotel where we worked, and my last night there before I left for Israel. Remember that Jewish family from Zurich, at the restaurant there in Bowness? I was to leave the next day for London to fly to Israel. When they heard what I was going to do, they not only insisted I visit them after the war, but they also tipped me fifty quid. They were proud of me. They meant it. They really wanted me to visit. And so the Swiss nurse at the kibbutz was the second address for me in Switzerland someday. I had nothing to do with the Swiss nurse except being friends. I was already with the Israeli girl by the time I got to know her. She had just moved in when the Israeli girl made her move on me."

"So is Switzerland where you went after you left Israel? I know it isn't, because you went to Frankfurt. Not to here but to damn West Germany, in the dead of winter, during an economic downturn due to the Arab oil boycott. You got a job at a U.S. military base petrol station."

I loved her memory.

"You're right there, Gail. I did get a job in

Frankfurt. I couldn't go back to the Lakes because all the hotels were closed, since it wasn't tourist season anymore. You know that. You're not being fair. I wanted to see you more than anything, but I had no money. They don't pay on a kibbutz. I wanted to travel around the world and check out some of the addresses I'd gotten at the hotel in Bowness. I thought maybe I could get a job in South Africa. The guy that gave me his address in Johannesburg told me I probably could, that there was even a large, prosperous Jewish community there. But 'probably' didn't cut it, since I was broke. I hoped to go to Kenya, where a couple I'd met owned a safari outfit, and then from there on to South Africa. But again, how do I get a visa for all these places when I have no money? So I went down to Elat on the Red Sea, hoping to get work in the copper mines down there. The Biblical ones. They still get copper from them all these millennia later. But the mines were still closed even though the war had ended. And they were shooting a movie about Moses down there, too, starring Burt Lancaster, but the movie also was still shut down because of the war. Then I met a couple of girls from Chicago, who told me U.S. military bases often hire, especially in Frankfurt. And since I'm a U.S. citizen, even a vet, I thought I might find work there."

Somehow Gail seemed to be checking me out. As if unanswered questions from those days so many years ago needed to be fulfilled.

"And luckily," I continued, "I did find work at the Air Force base next to the Frankfurt *flughafen*—you know, their airport. Thank God. El Al, the Israeli airline, had lost my backpack. Luckily, I was dressed warmly and hand-carried my sleeping bag. I was so broke. I had fifty bucks left after traveling around Israel and buying the airfare to Frankfurt. That included the twenty *Deutsch Marks* El Al gave me for having lost my backpack, or my bankroll wouldn't even have been that. I couldn't even afford a youth hostel. I slept on the ice in a little forest near the Air Force base."

She eased into a sympathetic smile and touched my hand again.

"At first I was pumping gas on the air base. Pumping gas during an oil shortage from the boycott. Can you beat that?"

"Only you, Jericho," she bragged. "You are such a survivor. Only you could waltz into a foreign country, naked and penniless, and find a job that shouldn't even exist. Is this the Jew, the Davy Crockett Texan, or the Marine in you? Had to be a combination of all three to pull that off. And all else you did, going around the world later on. Without me."

I adored the hero worshipping going on, but it embarrassed me.

"Gail, I would have loved to share my adventures with you, all that I did after I left you. But you would have never lived that kind of life." I hoped that was obvious enough to her that she didn't feel insulted.

So," I continued. "There I was in Frankfurt. And that's not all that far from Bern or Zurich. So I went down and visited both of those Swiss addresses from there. The family in Zurich was special because I had met them in the Lakes and they were Jewish. The nurse was special because we met during the war. In each place, they took me all over, at least in their general vicinity. The family took me to Luzern, and we took a cable car up to Mount Pilatus. They showed me the beautiful church there on the lake, too, and the medieval bridge. And the nurse in Bern took me to Interlaken and the Berner Oberland, their part of the Alps, you know. God, it is beautiful there, especially Grindelwald. I was just flabbergasted. It's like guardian angels live in Switzerland and keep it fresh and clean. And Bern isn't even a quarter million people, this quaint little city that's the capital of Shangri-La. I've seen Rome and Paris and London and Vienna. But I loved Bern over all of them. And the Aare River runs through it. The clock tower. The market. Parliament building. On the way back to her apartment from the mountains, my friend had us float in the current of the Aare River. All the way to Bern. Then we took a bus back to where she'd left her car by the river, at the point where we started floating. Then we hiked in the woods and the mountains. That's their national sport. Hiking. Can you believe it? I swore, 'Someday I'm going to live here, in Bern, Switzerland.' And now I do."

"So, you didn't have sex in the mountains and forests?" she asked while teasing me with a wink.

I laughed. Her wink was a good sign. Like I was off the hook. Maybe.

"I really didn't, I swear. She was never interested in me that way. Not romantically. She was engaged to be married. To a doctor. I met him. Her father was a doctor, too. She wouldn't have a Marine Jewish cowboy anyway. I was part of the adventure of the war to her. A great memory. Anyway, we've all stayed in contact, the family in Zurich, and the nurse and her husband in Bern, all through the years. The nurse and her husband even came to visit me in Texas. And I kept repeating how someday I'm going to live in Bern, Switzerland, the most beautiful city I'd ever seen. Well, her husband knew people. And he knew people in the Swiss government. They had a big shortage of COBOL programmers. You know, the computer language. And I know COBOL, but I hadn't been a programmer in years. I went to visit them for Christmas last year. Christmas in Switzerland! I just flipped out. The snow, the chocolate drinks, the roasted chestnuts, the bratwurst, the beer, the icy forests. I swore again I was going to live there someday. My last day there, the doctor arranged a meeting with me and the foreign office. *Bundesamtfuerauslaenderfragen.* That's what they call the foreign office. I didn't have a suit. I hadn't brought a resume. The interview went well, but who could imagine I'd get the job? But I did get it. I went home and gave my job notice in Houston, then took the next plane out."

She eased into a smile and reached over to rub my cheek, as if I'd passed some test.

"And here we are," she said.

"And here we the hell are."

She looked me more intensely in the eyes. As if bearing down.

"I despised that war in Vietnam," she blurted out to my bewilderment. "And you joined the Marines to go. You. The most sensitive person, male or female, I've ever met. It goes against the grain of all you're supposed to believe about these goons that go fight, especially a war like that. Is this some karma to torture me with? That I feel this way and fall for you who believes so strongly in doing just exactly things like that war?"

"Maybe it's not karma as much as a growing pain for you," I answered back.

"Not only is it somehow karma, growing pain variety or not, but karmic in that here we are together somehow from you having done that. If you hadn't been this loyal patriot doing his duty, you may well have never sown those wild oats that you did after you got out of the Marines. If no war, then no Marines for you. You'd just have gone to university and come out a clerk or whatever, settled down with some Jewish girl. But instead, you got out of the Marines, got antsy, wanted to see the world, meandered to England, and wound up in the Lakes. With me there as if waiting for you—karma, karma, karma. If you hadn't joined when you did, and gotten out when you did, we'd have never met, never been an us. What made you come to the Lakes, as a matter of fact? That's what I want to hear. The Lakes. Probably the most special place either of us ever experienced. With some cosmic karma waiting for us, in particular. Explain to me how this happened, and take me with you, figuratively and romantically speaking, in your explanation. Let's relive our days together as you narrate our encounter in the Lakes. Our meant-to-be days together, this time in our cosmic trip—let's never let go of them."

Chapter 3

When I got out of the Marines in the spring of 1973, I returned to my daddy's farm. I needed to go back to my roots. There was turmoil in the land because of the Vietnam War and the accompanying animosity by so much of our generation toward the politicians, but also toward those of us who served. I needed to feel productive again. To help on the farm made me feel worthwhile and nurtured. Appreciated.

The political scandal called Watergate was going on then, too. Even as I was on the farm trying to heal from the war, I had to endure more news reports about how the country I fought for was corrupt. I had to watch everything I patriotically loved rot before my eyes. By late July, after the grain harvest, I was restless. As the cotton harvest began, I wanted to get away even though I was needed. I stuffed my clothes and gear into my Marine combat backpack, attached a sleeping bag to it, and rolled around it my Marine field raincoat, what we called a poncho, and my Marine overcoat. I would wear my Marine combat boots and use my Marine fatigue jacket as a pillow when I camped out at night. I felt ready for anything. I didn't know where I was going, but I was starting now.

My best friend from college days was working on his doctorate at my alma mater, Texas A&M. I hitched a ride to see him. If anything was spiritually nourishing to me, it was the brotherhood so many of us from there had felt since our college days.

"Hey, hoss," my friend Jim said to me as we sat on his beat-up old couch in his studio apartment in the Northgate section of College Station, the town where A&M is located. Jim brought back good memories, and I felt better just seeing him. His scrawny, muscular, cowboy body with accompanying West Texas drawl had me relaxed and at home instantly.

"I just got back from India a few months ago," he said before spitting snuff into his empty longneck beer bottle. "You met my roommate when you visited me a few years ago, before they shipped you off to Nam. That Indian guy. He just finished his PhD and went back home to Delhi. He talked me into tagging along. I thought, 'What the hell.' All my old Cadet Corps buddies here at A&M went to Vietnam, or Europe, or at least someplace else in the States. 'I've never been out of Texas. Now's the time to do it if I'm ever going to do it,' I decided. 'I'll get my doctorate and spend the rest of my life behind a desk if I don't do something adventurous now.' "

Jim spit the last grains of his dip into the empty beer bottle before placing it on the lamp table next to him. Perhaps as a courtesy to me, he'd never let dipping or chewing interfere with our conversations before.

"The reason I'm bringing this up to you," he continued, "is that we flew to Luxembourg, then took a train to London. From there we took a bus to a place up near the Scottish border, a National Trust area, sort of like our National Park system, to a place called the Lake District, the most beautiful place I've ever seen. I know that's not saying much for the likes of me, but it had these green rolling hills. Sheep grazed on them, and they were fenced in by these old stone barrier fences. I felt I was back in primordial paradise. Wordsworth used to live there. They called him the Laureate of the Lakes, meaning of the Lake District of England. Charles Dickens and Beatrix Potter lived there, too. There's these old stone cottages and churches in the towns and villages. The churches have cemeteries on the grounds. I thought I walked into a lullaby. These rolling hills collect rain and pour that rain into a system of lakes. On the biggest lake, Lake Windermere, is where the tourist places are."

"The Lake District?" I asked, trying to sear the place into my brain. "Do you have a ballpoint pen or something I can write with, and a piece of paper? I want to remember the stuff you're telling me."

"Don't worry about remembering all this stuff," Jim said. "I'll write it down for you myself. Just listen."

I nodded to assure him I was all ears.

"Me and my Indian buddy worked as waiters in one of the fancy hotels in the Lake District. Illegally, no less. I would never have done this if my buddy hadn't worked there back when he went to Oxford. He took summers off and would go up to the Lakes and work as a waiter. They're screaming for help in the summertime. Hoss, the month of August is upon us. You're burning daylight. Get your ass to New York. You can get cheap flights out of Kennedy with Icelandic Airways. You have a stopover in Reykjavik. You can pretend you're excited about seeing a small frozen island no one but Vikings wanted to live in. Take a picture and then forget you ever saw the place. When you get to Luxembourg, go across northern

France—don't bother with Paris, they're rude to Americans there—and keep going until you get to Calais. Take the hovercraft across the English Channel to the white cliffs of Dover, and keep on going until you get to London. From there you can take a bus, or if you're on a shoestring budget you take the underground—that's their subway system—through London until you get to the expressway headed north. From there, it's a beeline to the Lake District. People catch rides with trucks. The Brits call them lorries. They're friendly people, these truck drivers, and they're bored. They'll get you to the Lakes if you entertain them with stories about wrestling alligators or whatever. In your case, you probably don't have to make stories up."

I never wrestled an alligator, but I didn't have to make up many stories of my days growing up in rural Texas, that was for sure.

"You're leaving tomorrow morning after we eat breakfast," Jim instructed. "I'm sick of you already anyway," he said with a laugh. "That's where you're going, if what you want to do is get away. The Lake District. Got it? Best days of your life are waiting for you, starting tomorrow. You'll never look back. Tomorrow is the first day of the rest of your life."

I hitchhiked from College Station through East Texas, Arkansas, Tennessee, Virginia, Maryland, Pennsylvania, then New Jersey, and on into New York City. The scenery was breathtaking all the way, not to mention the colorful backgrounds of many of the drivers who picked me up along the way. Often the radio blasted as we drove, and no matter what kind of music preference anyone had, bluegrass hits or folk music was included by all types of radio stations. Songs of the piney woods would play, or songs of the open road. I felt like the star of the show with the radio playing my musical score. I loved the South. But even the Yankee states were beautiful, though I felt guilty admitting it. And their radio stations played the music my life seemed to live, just as much as the Southern stations.

I was doing the right thing. I could feel it. Something real, even though like a dream, was happening to me now. I wasn't going to think about America anymore. I was going to see the world and put a reset on my life, beginning with the Lake District of England. The thought innervated me. After high school, it had excited me to get out of my hometown and go to college. Joining the Marines had been an even bigger excitement. The Marines opened up a whole new world for me, dangerous and depressing as it could be at times. But that only made me want more of the world now. Much more.

When I arrived at JFK airport, after I got my ticket to Luxembourg on Icelandic Airways, I just walked around. With each new airline section, I pictured being in that part of the world. Air India. Air Zambia. China Airlines. Qantas. I could see myself visiting and living in every continent, every country.

Icelandic Airways was the airline of the backpacking crowd, guys like me, not jetsetters so much as adventurers. Free spirits. Free spirits on a shoestring budget. Iceland, the Bahamas, and Luxembourg somehow skirted regulated airfare. The renegades of the airways. These countries and their airlines got past the unions, too. I was game. It meant cheap products—in this case, airfare. I couldn't afford to buy, otherwise. I liked the thought of it, and the feel of it, and my limited budget loved it even more.

Our stopover in Iceland was brief, but long enough for me to disembark and spend a couple of hours in the countryside. Which I did. It was noontime, and I took a bus to somewhere. I got off at the first small village and walked around it and through it. There was a hill on the edge of town, and I walked to the base of it. The wind was strong, and the air was cold. Not freezing, but cold enough I needed my Marine fatigue jacket. It was early August and already this cold. How did these people stay alive?

The weather in Luxembourg when I arrived, however, was brilliant and sunny. I was in Europe. I wanted to pinch myself. I loved the place already.

I found the road outside the airport that was on the way to France. I stuck out my thumb and let my luck begin. Everything, even getting stuck in God knows where, excited me. I was in control of my destiny.

Somewhere in the countryside past Paris and on the road to Calais, I got let out at a spot where there were two Scottish girls with red hair so bright it hurt my eyes. Their anemically pale white skin had blotches of big red freckles. I, for courtesy, walked past them so they could catch a ride before me. I could hear them talking and giggling about me with their sharp Celtic accents. That made my day.

Was I going to love everything? Common sense said not. But I didn't care. I was ready for anything.

Every place so far I'd encountered before only in the news, in movies, or through books. There really was a world out there, and I was passing through it.

Then there it was, the English Channel. Time after time, this bit of ocean had kept England from being invaded by treacherous armies. And on the other side of it was England itself: the Mother Country. Big Ben, the Thames, Shakespeare, Newton, the Magna Carta, George III, the Beatles. And the Lake District. It took hours to cross the Channel by regular ferry boat, but only about an hour by hovercraft, which Jim had made special note to mention to me. These were boats supported by a perimeter of giant inner-tube-looking things. It was propelled by thrusts of air pressure exploding from outlets in the boat, allowing it to skim along the surface like a skipped rock instead of plowing through the water. Even though the hovercraft was more expensive, I took it. I was in a hurry, and it was getting dark.

Before long, I could see the white cliffs of Dover. Was I ever going to get past the awestruck stage? They were beautiful, they were historic, and they were mine. Metaphorically mine. As soon as I disembarked from the craft onto the highway leading to London, a tour bus stopped to pick me up. Free of charge. The driver saw this hitchhiker, me, and kindly stopped to give me a lift even though I hadn't put my thumb out asking for a ride. It was like a sign of approval from God. By now I believed this.

I didn't arrive in London until late in the evening. The bus driver told me which underground to take to get to Victoria Station. By the time I got there, most of the buses and trains going out of town were finished for the night. Nor could I take Jim's advice and ride the underground far enough to get me out of the city. So I found an empty bench at the train station and lay down to sleep, using my backpack for a pillow. I had a headache, but it was my first night in Europe. My first night in England. Not even a headache was going to spoil it.

"Are you going to hog the entire bench?" a sweet-sounding voice asked me after a few minutes, before I could get to sleep.

I looked up. I wanted to pretend it was an angel. But it was better than that. She was real. A short, freckled, redheaded girl stood over me with a playful scowl on her face. She wore blue jeans and a collared, long-sleeved shirt. I immediately sat up.

"Sorry," I replied. "I have a headache, and the underground is closing."

"The underground doesn't close this early, silly," she said with a laugh.

"Well, I just got here and don't know my way around. I'm headed for the Lake District and was told to take the underground until the end. The one that is near the expressway."

"Well, for sure you can't get out of London in time to get a decent lift. You're going to the Lakes? You won't even make it tomorrow unless you get good rides. Are you American? I'm thinking so, by your accent, but yours is a harsh accent."

I smiled. I was proud of my accent.

"I'm from Texas," I explained.

Her mouth flew open, displaying pure astonishment.

"Texas! My goodness! You *are* a long way from home. And here I am in Victoria Station with a bloke from Texas. I never even dreamed this day would come."

We stared at one other for a moment, at a loss for words. Paralyzed in intrigue.

"So," she said with a giggle. "Back to my original premise. Are you going to hog the entire bench here? I have an hour's wait for the train to Manchester. That's where I live now. I'm a student at the university there. I'd love to share my time, and your bench, with a cowboy from Texas. You are a cowboy, right? From your attire and your speech?"

I nodded that I was as I made room for her, placing my backpack on the ground while I turned my body to sit leaning against the back of the bench.

She sat right next to me, her body touching mine.

Without saying a word, she reached into her shirt pocket and handed me a piece of gum after taking one for herself. A smile spread over her face while she waited for me to take the piece she offered.

"I'd rather have an aspirin," I said. "I can't believe I didn't bring any with me."

"I have aspirin in me rucksack," she answered.

She reached down over her small backpack and pulled out a clear, plastic bottle. Again, without saying a word, she handed me two aspirin.

"You don't have water to swish it down, do you, mate?" she asked as I struggled to open the bottle top.

I shook my head no. She smirked and shook her head likewise, wearing a look of pathetic sympathy. She then pulled out a metal canteen from her backpack, handed it to me, and watched me take the aspirin for my headache.

"Did you just arrive from Texas?" she asked as I handed her back her aspirin and canteen.

I nodded yes. "By way of Luxembourg," I said.

"And now, here I am in London, where I've met my first friend."

"Really?" she swooned. "I'm your first friend here. Is that fab? I love it."

She reached down excitedly again into her backpack and pulled out a small book. In it was a ballpoint pen, which she pulled out to hand to me, along with the book.

"Here," she said. "Give me your address, and I'll give you mine. I want to hear about all your adventures in the Lakes or wherever. My name is Liz, by the way."

With that she grabbed my hand to shake, as if to seal a vow perhaps. I also had an address book, which I gave her for her name and address. She quickly thumbed through it and saw that it was empty. Her smile broadened.

"I'll be the first to fill in an address," she gloated.

I nodded and held in a laugh. She went to the R's to write her name, but I stopped her.

"No, write your address under L. For Liz, your first name. I'll remember first names more than I will last names."

"Clever boy," she said as she scribbled her information in my address book after I finished writing mine in hers.

"Your name is Jericho?" she asked, after inspecting all I had written, when we gave back our respective address books. "That's a strange name, isn't it? I never heard of such before. So, Jericho, me lad, you will write me, won't you?"

"For sure," I said. "I like the thought of having new friends. Adventure ones."

She leaned over and kissed me on the cheek. We

stared at one another for a moment until the stares turned into gazes. I wanted to kiss her on the lips and could feel she did me also. I wasn't shy, but I was a guy, and guys always do the kissing, as if imposing themselves on an innocent damsel was all right. So I hoped she would initiate the longed-for kisses, but instead, she turned away.

"How's your head?" she asked as she returned her address book to her backpack.

"Still there," I said.

"My train's not for another hour. Why don't you lie back down on the bench like I found you? But lay your head on me lap. I'll massage your neck. You'll feel better soon."

I did as she suggested. Her warm and tender fingertips stroked my neck and forehead. My headache was gone in minutes, but I didn't tell her. I wanted more as I took a few minutes' nap.

"Tell me about Texas," she said once I opened my eyes. "You hear so much."

I sat back up next to her and thought for a moment.

"It's a big state. Size of France. More cattle than people, but a lot of people too. And oil."

"I know all those things. What was it like to grow up there?"

"I grew up on a farm. We had citrus, corn, vegetables, but mostly cotton. Cotton was the big cash crop. So much so, the U.S. government paid us money not to grow too much of it. To stabilize the market."

"Seriously? You were paid not to grow cotton?"

"We grew a lot of it. We got paid to not grow only it."

"No cattle?" she asked with disappointment. "You

said you were a cowboy."

"We had a few head," I replied.

"Is growing cotton really such hard work?" she asked. "I hear incredible stories. *Gone With the Wind*-type stories."

"Even with all the mechanization there are hundreds of acres to deal with. Plowing, planting, hoeing, cultivating, harvesting. By harvest time, it's summer and so hot and dusty. You've got boll weevils, too. With cotton, you pick it the first time by hand, then again by machine after you've defoliated it. Then you cut it down—by machine, but again it's so hot and dusty, and the stalk cutter blows the dust into clouds, and then some of the cotton stalks, which are like wood by then, get shot at you by the cutter blade. That's the worst part of the whole cotton season. Then you disc the fields, then plow. You use a breaking plow, which goes deep into the soil and turns the ground over the cotton roots to put them deeper into the soil. But you have to drive so slowly and can only get a few feet plowed per sweep. You do that from late summer on into autumn."

"My goodness, Jericho. How do you put up with all of that?"

"You feel productive. I hated the work. I used to count the days until school started. But actually, I loved the farm. I felt good about life there. About being productive. About working hard, even as a discipline. And most of the summer you're working seven days a week, for up to fourteen hours a day. I loved it. I hated it but I loved it. I love overcoming hardship and strengthening from it. It adds to your self-confidence in the process. I hate city kids. They're spoiled brats. No wonder the country's going to crap. They don't make the connection to anything. They think everything comes from a store. And they look at me like I'm some hick coolie. Like what I do is beneath them. They think I just do farming because I'm too stupid to do anything else. But farming's a life of its own, a culture called agriculture. To hell with city slickers."

I considered how I must sound and looked over at her apologetically.

"I don't really hate city kids. I'm sorry. But life can be too easy, you know. You don't know the meaning of sacrifice when it's that easy, and you don't want to know. Hick coolies like me are a reminder of not wanting to know, and so we're fair game to belittle. Sometimes it gets personal. Sorry I expressed it."

"No, I understand, Jericho. England is so into socialism now. No one wants to be a coolie here, for sure. They want rights and security."

"Cyrus the Great had it down," I mused. "He didn't want his empire ruled from the plush parts of his empire but from the arid, rough places. Your environment produces you. If it's too easy, you're too soft. Hard environments can overwhelm, but that's all you hear these days. Everyone is overwhelmed if things ain't easy. What we need, Cyrus understood—we need challenges in our life. That's for sure. It's focus. Hard environments create durable people."

I shrugged and glanced at her again, embarrassed at how I was on a talkative roll.

"My train is approaching, Jericho. I loved meeting you. Do please write to me. I want to keep up with your adventures. I live a drab sort of life. Not complaining, but let me know what I'm missing, if you don't mind."

She picked up her backpack, and I walked her to her train. She grabbed my hand to hold it as we walked. I melted inside but tried not to show it.

"*Ciao*, Jericho," she said with affection and a longing look.

She tiptoed enough to kiss me on the lips. Before I could return the kiss she broke away and walked the last steps to her train, stopping one last time to smile at me before boarding.

I barely slept that night, on the bench, as I thought about her. I loved Europe. I adored England. I was ready for more.

Chapter 4

It was a piece of cake to get to the expressway the next morning. This pleasantly surprised me, as I was ready to rumble with the struggles of the road. Adventure wasn't hard at all. Why didn't more people do this, I wondered.

"You needn't stand by the road with your thumb out, mate," a young, long-haired, fellow hitchhiker informed me during our conversation. "Get yourself a lift to a weigh station on the express. A bunch of lorries there. Just walk up to them and tell them where you're going. You'll get to the Lakes in no time. They'll love helping someone from Texas."

I nodded my head as a thank you. His advice reinforced what my friend Jim had said to me back in Texas, that not only were the truck drivers willing to give rides, but they went for long distances at a whack.

"It's easy wrestling alligators," I lied to the lorrie driver who picked me up at a weigh station. Following Jim's advice again, I decided to practice up on my stories to entertain my captive audiences on these hitchhiking journeys. "You get in a boat—a piroque we call them back home. That's Cajun French. I'm not Cajun, but I learned the ropes from them. You have to look hard in the swamps to find an alligator. It's often shadowy dark, and the alligators are mostly submerged below the water's surface. You can see their noses sticking out a tad, and they make little riffle waves when they paddle. You get good at spotting them after a while."

"You never been in no swamp," the driver scoffed. It was amazing how they looked like truck drivers back home. Pot-bellied, grizzled, five o'clock shadows. British drivers didn't wear caps much, though. "That's Davy Crockett stuff." The driver laughed, enjoying the story anyway. "You're pullin' me bleedin' leg."

"I'm serious," I answered, straight-faced. I then stared him down as if in shock he didn't believe me. "You ever been to Texas?" I asked.

He looked at me, still skeptical, then returned his attention to the highway. "Go on, then," he said. "Tell me how to wrestle a bloody alligator." A giant smile broke out on his face. He was enjoying this.

"They don't attack the boat, the piroque. Some of the Cajuns have a rope with a loop. They drop it into the water in front of the alligator, then ease it to the alligator's nose and slip it quickly over the mouth. It's all over then. Strong and mean as an alligator is with its ferocious jaws when it bites, the jaws pretty much use gravity to open up with. Almost no muscles used to open. That's their downfall. Once you've secured the noose, just tighten it, and they are putty in your hands."

He looked over at me, wearing another skeptical sneer.

"But you get bored with that after a while," I continued. "Too easy. You make a game out of it. Like a rodeo or something. Most people carry a Bowie knife, just to be safe. But all you really need is your rope, if you do it right."

"And you do it right, I take it." The driver snorted.

"It's not that hard," I replied. "It's not even that scary, once you've done it a couple of times. With your knife wedged in your belt, and rope in hand, you jump onto the back of the alligator, and before he jolts away, you secure that loop around his snout. If you're wrestling with him, you don't want to take any chances. Just give it a couple of secure wraps around his snout, and you've got him. He's more worried about getting away than fighting you. I always crawl back into the boat before he dives. Wrap the other end of the rope around a peg in the boat or the boat seat, and he ain't going nowhere. Then just paddle him to shore. You can get a lot of money for an alligator hide. The meat's good, too. Always a market for that. But just the meat from the upper part of the tail."

"And you expect me to believe you do this for a livin' in Texas, do you? I thought Texans herded cattle. I heard you call them doggies."

"Yeah, we have a ranch. Five hundred head of cattle. But we have swamps around, too. It's always good to have another source of income available. Wrestling steers and alligators is fun even without the money. Two different styles of wrestling, but both of them are fun. And you can make a good living."

"So if I come visit you someday, you're goin' to show me how to do this, are you?"

"Even a lorrie driver can do this stuff," I said straight-faced. "It's overrated. People think it's dangerous. Hardly anyone gets killed. You get a few scars, but those you wear like badges of honor. Shows what you're made of."

"Show me a scar, then."

I unlashed my combat boot, pulled down my sock,

and showed him a long pale scar I got when I was a teenager, from stepping on a broken beer bottle.

The driver inspected it and then checked me out. He almost seemed to believe me. "Was that from an alligator or a steer horn?" he asked.

"From taking down a wild hog with a pocket knife, actually. But that's another story. We have a lot of feral hogs around, too, and they're a pest to our crops, but good to eat. You don't get much money for them, but every little bit helps."

"So, tell me, then, matey, what does wild hog taste like?"

"I don't know. Never ate one. I'm Jewish."

"You're tellin' me a Yid goes around trappin' and killin' wild hogs and can't eat the bleedin' meat?"

"I suppose we aren't supposed to even touch them. I don't remember. We didn't have a rabbi back home when I was growing up. Anyway, a dead hog is a dead hog, and they bring in extra money. Not to mention the hides."

He looked out the window to his side and began to howl with laughter. "Yes, sir. You're worth the ride there, matey," he bellowed. "I haven't had so much fun in all me days behind the wheel. That's good. That's good. Worth the pick-up, you were."

He looked back at me and held out his hand to shake.

"I like you, son. We need more of your kind here in Britain. Too many slouches here in the bleedin' welfare state. Can't make a bob these days, taxes are so high. We need more Cajuns and cowboys. I almost believe your stories, but I don't want to hear if you're joshin' me. It's too much fun goin' along with it. I'll be damned. Yes I will. I'll just plain be damned."

I hoped I could tell this story as well the next time I tried. This might work out, I decided.

At the lorry stop where the trucker dropped me, as I was looking for another lorry ready to leave, an old Volkswagen van pulled up beside me.

"Looks like you're needing a lift there," a guy with long blond hair to his shoulders said to me from the passenger side of the front.

"I'm heading to the Lake District," I explained.

"The Lakes, now," the driver of the van said. He also had long blond hair to his shoulders but wore a shortly cropped beard, in addition. "That's a ways yet. I see why you're checking out the lorries. Where are you from, with that accent? It's like out of a Western movie."

"I'm from Texas," I replied.

Broad smiles came onto both their faces.

"Somehow you look like a Texan," the guy from the passenger side said. "Long and tall, wearing boots and blue jeans. Those aren't cowboy boots, I suppose."

"We're not going too far," the driver apologized. "Just to Blackpool. About an hour from here. It's heading north like you want. Would you like a ride? It's getting late afternoon when we get there. We can put you up, if you need. We live on a commune. We have space for you."

A commune. I had never been to one. I doubted they liked alligator stories, but I would think of something, I was sure.

"I'd like a ride. Thanks for the offer."

Instead of entertaining them, I preferred just looking out the window at the scenery as we drove.

England was so green, even more so than France had been, greener than any place I'd ever seen. All that rain I heard about must be true.

"So did you like the Marines, then, after you joined?" the driver asked me along the way as we talked. I was grateful to get past the Texas questions everyone routinely asked. Though I was a bit leery to talk about my Marine experiences with guys from a commune, after all my encounters with the Age of Aquarius back home, I was seasoned on the subject by now. The guy in the passenger side was looking at me intently, waiting for my answer.

"I loved the Marines," I replied.

"Is it as hard as they say?" the driver asked. "We hear all sorts of stories."

"I don't know what you heard, but it was hard enough. That's why I joined, though. I wanted hard."

"Why would that be?" the driver asked.

"Challenge," I answered. "To be stronger."

"Do you suppose such grueling training and violence really makes you stronger?" the passenger-side man asked. "Have you read the *Bhagavad Gita*? Or the *Upanishads*?"

"Parts," I replied. "And the Sermon on the Mount too. Very moving."

Both men from the commune nodded in approval.

"Isn't that inner strength?" the passenger-side man asked.

"Yes it is," I replied. "Turn the other cheek and all is certainly inner strength. At least if you do it from inner strength and not just following some doctrine. Rules-to-nirvana stuff, or dancing by the spiritual numbers. If you really have that strength and wisdom, then you're on your way to enlightenment, I suppose."

They glanced at me as if wondering what I was talking about.

"And I believe in diplomacy," I continued. "But if that fails, then the rest of the story."

"Which is?" they both asked in unison.

"Outfight them," I replied. "Violently, if need be."

"And what would that get you?" the man on the passenger side asked.

"Kept alive."

"At what cost?" he inquired further.

"At whatever cost required."

"Evil doesn't overcome evil," the driver said.

"Force overcomes force," I replied.

"Love is a force."

"If you've got enough of it, great. But if I don't have enough of it, I'll use my fists. Or whatever it takes."

"I don't know what kind of world we'll have then."

"Better than the one my enemies have in mind."

"Are all Texans like you?" the man in the passenger side asked with a grin.

"Texas cowboys are, for sure," I answered.

"Will you feel uncomfortable with us at the commune?" the driver asked.

"I'll be okay. I've never been to one. I'm looking forward to it."

They nodded approval.

We reached the ocean after a while. Blackpool was one of the primary beach resort areas in England, the men from the commune informed me on the way. People were swimming in late afternoon while the air seemed crisp for summer, to my Texan sensibilities.

England was so far north. Surely the water was cold. How did they not have pneumonia, I wondered.

"We live nearby," the driver informed me. "We'll be there just in time to eat. Perhaps you would like to shower, too."

I smiled that I would.

I had seen the movie *Easy Rider* when it came out. There was a scene about a commune in New Mexico. The movie *Alice's Restaurant* had some parts about communes, too. That was as close as I had ever come to one until now.

When we arrived, they showed me my quarters in a small cottage on the grounds. There were several such cottages. The cottage had several rooms and a hallway. I wasn't sure of the living arrangements and didn't ask. After the guys showed me my room, they left me to myself.

Shortly, I heard a knock on my door. I opened it, and a young girl I took to be in her twenties, with long black hair, welcomed me with a smile and a plate of spaghetti. She wore a black cotton blouse with ruffled shoulder sleeves and a black skirt that almost touched the floor.

"Hello," she said with a warm smile. "I heard you would be spending the night with us here. I'm sorry you missed the communal meal. We would love to know you. We have plenty of leftovers, if this plate of spaghetti doesn't satisfy you. There is a shower at the end of the hallway. Stick your head out of your door, and I'll point to it."

It was at a far end of the cottage, taking what might have been the space of two bedrooms.

"And at the other end are the toilets. So help

yourself. Do you need anything? I'll leave you to yourself for a while and check on you in perhaps an hour or so. Is that all right with you?"

"I'm fine. Thank you."

There were two spring beds in the room. They were small, each enough for one person, and I hoped long enough to fit my six-foot-three frame. There were also two desks, each with a chair. I sat at one of the desks while I ate my spaghetti. I felt awkward. I was grateful to them for their kindness, but I felt out of place.

After I finished eating, I grabbed a change of clothing from my backpack and prepared to shower. I didn't have any shampoo or soap but assumed they did in the shower stalls. I would hand wash my clothes while I had the chance also, with the same bar of soap that I used for my shower, as I had brought with me only three sets of clothes, total.

It was an open shower with four shower heads, each with a soap dish attached to the walls just under the shower heads. I laid my dirty clothes on a chair near the doorway and hung my clean change of clothes on one of the hooks attached to the door. I had been in the shower for only a few minutes when the door opened and in walked a naked man and naked woman, each appearing to be in their twenties. It took me by surprise, but under the circumstances, I wasn't flabbergasted by any of it and managed to not show emotion. I quickly managed a smile of greeting as if I was an old hand at communal living.

"Hello," each of them said in a polite, friendly manner. "We heard we had a guest," the man said. "Don't feel rushed by us. There's plenty of room for all of us. Carry on."

"Is it all right if I hand wash my clothes while I'm in here?" I asked.

"Of course it is," the girl answered. "But we have a washing machine in the communal mess and laundry house. It's near the entrance to the grounds as you came in. But you're welcome to hand wash, also. It's up to you."

They were gentle with one another as they washed themselves thoroughly, one minute each washing his or her own body, then trading off to wash the other. I felt silly with all the questions that raced through my mind about the scene, but to me it advertised well for a commune.

The girl who had greeted me earlier in my room stuck her head through the doorway of the shower room and looked at me as I washed my dirty blue jeans.

"There you are," she said. "I'll be in later to say good night to you in your room, to make sure you're all right."

"Sure," I said, ready to blush, as if suddenly it mattered to be seen naked around her.

After I finished washing, I wondered why I bothered to put on my clean clothes, because of my circumstances, but cultural momentum of past years held sway, and I did so.

I don't know if the awkwardness I felt caused my mood when I returned to my room or if it was just loneliness because of being away from home, but for the first time in my excursions, I felt melancholy.

Through the years, beginning in early boyhood, I had known a strong pull to be an artist. The first thing I ever remember wanting to be was an artist, the painter variety, a Van Gogh or a Rembrandt, though in my pre-school days I didn't know who they were. By second grade we had to draw in class, and it was then I realized just how badly I was fitted for that dream. Because I was lousy at drawing. Maybe the worst in the class. Even at a young age I understood that you didn't always get what you wanted, that some people are good at some things and other people aren't. But I turned out to be so horrible at drawing that it shocked and irritated me. I saw how good everyone's drawings were compared to mine. Until then, I had thought my pictures were ugly because I was young and awkward, that they were stiff from immaturity. I had been sure that when I got older my drawing ability would blossom. But it dawned on me that, with all the good artists in my second grade class, there was no growing into talent. End of story. Even in second grade some of the kids had beautiful drawings. Definitely not me.

It didn't make sense to me that I was this bad at drawing. Something inside insisted I was an artist. It turned out I was musically inclined, however. My father was a good singer, so I wasn't totally shocked when it turned out I was also. I so loved music, but assumed everyone did. The more I was exposed to music, the more my talent for it appeared. I could even write music. It was just there inside me. Songs came out. Songs became my expression. I was good with words, too.

When Elvis hit the world scene when I was little, I couldn't have cared less. But I did take notice that guys like Buddy Holly and Chuck Berry wrote their own songs. Then later I saw that The Beatles did also. But the one that really made me want to be a songwriter was Hank Williams. They called him the Hillbilly Shakespeare. He moved me like no other artist ever. I had to do that, somehow.

I didn't know how good I was at writing songs, or if I was good at all. I just knew I could write music, so I envisioned going to Nashville someday to find out how good I might be, but I never did. College, the Marines, the farm, and now this with the Lakes, happened to me, so I never sought out my dream.

Yet I kept writing songs. And on this night at the commune I needed expression. I was by myself and glad. I had a song to write. And then I'd have to find a way to remember it, since I had no cassette recorder or even a guitar to work it out.

This was a time when the words came out with the melody. As strong as my emotions were, I wasn't surprised. A pencil and several sheets of paper were in the desk drawer, and I got them out, hoping that with the words I jotted down the melody would be part of those words and I would remember it later on as I reread them.

In a few minutes there was a knock on the door. This irritated me, since I was in the middle of the song. I quickly went over the few words I had down already, to see if I was past the fumbling beginner stage. The song seemed clear to me as a whole, words with melody. So I got up and went to the door.

"Hello," said the girl who had been there before. "I hope I'm not disturbing you."

"Oh, no," I lied. "It's good to see you. Thanks for checking on me."

"I guess you have everything you need?"

"I'm fine."

"My name is Jill, by the way. I can't believe I didn't introduce myself already. None of us did, in our little cottage you share with us, and I didn't realize it until someone asked me your name a few minutes ago. 'Who's this tall Texan among us?' was the question. And while I'm apologizing, some of my communal cottage mates are busy putting our little tots to bed while some are in the communal dining room cleaning it up from supper. Since I already met you, I was elected to make you feel welcomed and not just a lodger-friend for the night."

"My name is Jericho. So our names both start with J. It's okay about not introducing yourself earlier. I came from nowhere, suddenly, with everyone finishing their day and preparing for the evening. Don't worry about it. I understand. I could have introduced myself too. We were in a muddle."

"Still, that's no excuse," she said. "You meet someone, you greet him, and you find out his name. But somehow we were too preoccupied to bother. I am terribly sorry at the stiffness of it all. If I was told your name when you came in from your ride here, I didn't catch it. Only that we had a Texan among us. Anyway, may I come in?"

"Yes, of course," I replied and made a mental note to leave the door open, just to prove everything going on in my room was peaceful.

"So have you ever been to a commune before?" she asked as she walked into the room. "Do they have any in Texas? I hope you don't mind me asking. I was just curious. You're probably curious about us, too."

"I'm sure there are communes in Texas," I answered. "They're all over the place in America, not just California, where it's supposed to be so hip and modern. One of the most successful I heard about is in conservative and traditional Dixie. Somewhere in Tennessee. Or at least they were successful last I heard. Seems like they're all struggling now. I don't know."

"It's a nice life," Jill said. "An alternative style. We take care of one another. Some of us work around the commune. We own and rent collectively about five acres, I guess. We farm a bit, raise our own veggies and chickens and such. We have a small tractor and a few implements. We sell things like maize, cheese, and eggs on the market. Some of us make pottery or embroider or knit. We have a couple that sing folk songs at a pub in Blackpool. If someone has a skill and gets a job, they might choose to work in town, too. They get to keep most of their money. We find that works out better. We all put into a communal pool some of what we make. And we're here for each other. It's nice."

I nodded as I tried to envision the life.

"Are you really a cowboy?" she asked. "I heard you had a nice talk on the ride here. You really impressed the guys you came in with."

"We raise a few head of cattle now and then on our family farm. We mostly raise crops, though. But it's rural Texas. Life on a farm or ranch is much the same in lifestyle and culture. I grew up in a farming area. Very rich soil and lots of water. You can make a decent living. There are a lot of farms in our area. I like that."

"You hear so many stories about Texas," she said. "So many movies set there. It's nice to meet someone from there. Do you mind if we sit while we speak, Jericho?"

"Oh, sure. Sorry. Yes, make yourself at home. It's

your home, not mine, anyway."

She walked over to the chair in front of the desk I had been using, while I sat on the edge of the bed in front of her.

"What do you intend to do in the Lakes? I was told you hoped to find work in a hotel there."

"I heard I could. One of my buddies back home did that. Even illegally."

"Illegal?" she mused. "Oh yes, I suppose so. We call it black labor. Same thing. I didn't think of it being illegal, even though it is. They often get you a work visa, so I'm not sure it's considered illegal then."

"I just got out of the Marines. I can't seem to make myself settle down. I want to see something else in life. Get out a bit. Even find myself. The Lakes is where I'll start."

"Find yourself?" she asked in a sympathetic tone. "Like I hear about Marines coming home from the war? Looking for their head or something?"

I nodded yes.

"It must have been hard," she sighed, just above a whisper. "We hear so many things."

I nodded yet again and shrugged.

"You don't want to talk about it, I can tell. I understand."

"It's okay. I can. But yeah, we'd just get into it. And there's a lot to explain that I don't even understand myself."

"Yes, quite. I can imagine, Jericho. We can talk about something else."

She laid her elbow on the desk, which rustled the piece of paper with the first verse of my song lyrics. She turned to see about it and noticed the writing.

"Is that a poem?" she asked.

"I write songs," I answered self-consciously.

"Songs? Really? Marvelous! I would love to do such things. Do you mind if I read it?"

"It's not ready. I just got the first words out when you knocked."

"I don't want to impose on you, Jericho, but I'm intrigued. Please. I won't judge you. I understand it's not ready. I'm just curious is all. Is it all right if I read it?"

"Sure."

She read over the words as if studying them, then read them over again. Finally, she looked up at me.

"I haven't a clue what you just said in these lyrics, but I don't mean it in a bad way. I was expecting some singing-cowboy-type words. I guess Roy Rogers or something, but these are not that at all. Can you explain them? Please. I feel such an intruder, but please. I came in here just to be polite and a host, but now I really want to know you. No wonder one hears so much about Texans. And Marines. Please, help me; let's just talk. I'll be respectful. You said song lyrics. Are these just the words, or is there a melody to go with it?"

"Yes, there's a melody with them. They pretty much came together. Sometimes it happens that way. Usually, with me at least, I get a melody and a few words might come with it, and I have to wrestle with my emotions to get the rest out. Or I get a hook on its own and maybe later I can put a melody with it. But like now, sometimes the words come with the melody, if you can keep up with the words enough."

She smiled and shook her head. "Texans are not at all like they are portrayed. You look Texan, I suppose, however one is supposed to look, and you sound like one with your speech, and then there are your mannerisms, not to mention coming from a farm. But there is something else about you. Something not so Texan. Something about you is not like anybody."

She studied the words some more and then looked back at me.

"Now that I've already intruded, just for a special memory for me, can you sing these for me? I so wish you would." Suddenly, she sat upright, then stood up. "Wait, I play the guitar," she chirped. "Let me go get it. Let's work this song out together. This will be my special night indeed. I've never done such a thing."

"I'll do it," I said awkwardly. "But...don't tell the others. Let it just be you and me. I can relax around you. I'm relaxing already, but I'll get stiff inside if you drag anybody else into this. It needs to flow out from me while I relax. I'll get self-conscious if more show up."

"I won't tell a soul. I may have to explain about the guitar, but don't worry. I'll handle this. Give me just a moment."

She rushed out the door. As she did so, I walked over to read my words again, trying to picture what she saw in them, but also to get back into the song itself. The melody was miraculously still there inside me as I read the words.

Soon she returned with her guitar, a frisky energy exploding out of her as she sat back down on the chair.

"What key?" she asked. "I guess you don't know yet. I'll help you find it. Come on."

"I have a feeling it's in A minor. It doesn't sound like a major chord in my head. Or feel like it. May I borrow your guitar and check it out?"

"You know how to play?" she asked girlishly as she handed me her guitar. "Why not? Of course you do."

I sat back on the bed across from her. I formed the A minor chord and strummed it while humming the melody.

"Yeah, good, it's A minor. My favorite chord and progression."

"This is so much fun," she said with a giggle. "God sent you here somehow. Okay, do it, Jericho. Sing to me your own creation."

I strummed through the words to work out the song on the guitar. It all fit so well—words with music and melody, with my favorite progression—like I could only dream.

Canonized
The pain reminds
Love you hold inside is
Only heartache
Mm-mmm
Only heartache
Oh you
Only heartache.

More words found their way from me after I finished singing the first verse to her. I grabbed the pencil and paper from the desktop, and while standing over the paper next to her, I scribbled them out. Even a guitar rift oozed out with the melody.

I continued my song to her, this time opening with the rift.

Shattered dreams
Empty seeds

Pain to fill the needs
Only heartache
Oh you
Only heartache
Mm-mmm
Only heartache.

I grabbed the pencil again. The rephrase was making its way now. I hoped I could write so fast.

"Oh, Jericho," she swooned after I finished writing all the words and sang them to her. "I never had such a night. A song written right here in front of me like this! I love Texas now, but in ways no one has ever loved Texas, I bet. But Jericho, what does it mean? These words. What are they saying? What is bringing them out of you now? Did you have a girlfriend once? A soulmate? The love of your life and she's gone now and left 'only heartache'? Is that too easy? Is that too predictable? What's in there inside you, Jericho?"

"I don't know. But yes, there was someone in my past like that. And she did break my heart. I'm not saying that's what's in those words, even though it looks like it. It's just a mood. An imagery of feelings. And I guess she's the reference point or something in my feelings coming out. I don't know."

"Jericho," she said emphatically. "I know what a commune must look like to you in this age of ours. We don't hold Victorian rigidness here, for sure. But why I'm bringing this up is because I want to tear off my clothes now in front of you, to vamp you on that bed where you sit. But I can't and I won't. It's bad enough to tell you, but I want to be honest and bold. Even though I'm not married, there is a standard here. Loose by traditional measures, but still a trust involved that is important to me and this commune. A trust requiring nurture, not simply rules of etiquette, based on devotion and caring. I won't shatter that trust with my communal family. So I'll tell you about the chemistry inside me about you, then leave this room before I forget myself and make regrets. I will kiss you now. Passionately. And I'm not asking your permission."

With that she knelt in front of me while pulling me toward her by my neck and giving me the most forceful and passionate kiss of my entire life.

"And I want you to keep this guitar," she said. "As a remembrance. Don't you ever in your life forget me."

I spent another sleepless night thinking of a girl I met in England.

Chapter 5

It was night by the time I got to the village of Windermere, namesake of the lake it was on. Since Lake Windermere was the biggest of the lakes, it was where most of the commercial tourist enterprises lay. I was advised, by a girl who picked me up from nearby Kendal, to proceed on to Bowness-on-Windermere. Her soft accent was alluring, a genteel British one that seemed to make her words sound poetic as she spoke. Bowness, so she informed me, had some of the biggest hotels.

"Bowness is toward the middle of the lake on the eastern shore," she advised me. "You should start looking at hotels there and work your way on up to the top of the lake, at Ambleside. But you'll probably find work immediately. I worked there a summer, at The Old Britannia Hotel. That's the biggest hotel, and it's right by the pier where the tour boat docks. That's your best bet. Start there at that hotel. They were always looking for waiters—with all this unemployment in the country, and to have to plead for waiters! Beggars the imagination. That's the welfare state for you. But it's good for you while you're here. You're black labor and no one cares. You'll love Bowness. And they'll love having a Texas cowboy in their midst. You'll get big tips, and those don't get taxed. Even our small salary was taxed by over a fourth. Can you believe? All that so all our needs are taken care of by the state free of charge. Right. Free of charge. Vote for the government and get everything free. And get taxed into oblivion. The most expensive free in history. We see how that worked out."

I took a ferry boat on Lake Windermere, where the girl dropped me off, and it took me to the dock near The Old Britannia Hotel in Bowness, just like she said. I walked into the lobby, but not before leaving my backpack and guitar outside, to the side of the entrance door. I already looked like a bum, and my gear only made my appearance worse.

I wasn't sure how to go about asking for a job, except to just do it. So I walked up to the reception counter.

"Hello," I said, smiling nervously at a young and attractive female receptionist. She had long, brown, straight, flowing hair. Her smile in return was broad and warm.

"Good evening to you," she responded in a soft British accent. It wasn't harsh like the cockney accents in movies I had seen, nor as smooth as that of the girl from Kendal. "Are you in need of a room?"

"I'm in need of a job, to be honest," I said while trying to appear calm and confident.

Her eyes widened, as did those of the young receptionist standing next to her.

"You mean here?" she asked. "You would like to work for The Old Britannia? As a waiter, perhaps, or in our stillroom?"

"Whatever you've got," I replied.

The two receptionists leaned to whisper to one another. I heard mumbling.

"We do need waiters," the girl finally said to me. "Also for room service. Is this your first attempt to find employment in the Lakes? I mean this encounter with us is your first attempt?"

"Yes, ma'am."

She smiled widely with that.

"You called me ma'am," she said warmly. "I love that. No one ever calls me ma'am. Americans are cute—I assume you're American by your accent."

I smiled and nodded yes.

"Are you from the South?" she asked. "Isn't that common to say that in the South? Or am I just believing hearsay?"

"I'm from the South, yes, ma'am," I assured her, my confidence improving. "Texas."

"Texas," both girls said with glee. "You're from Texas?"

"Yes, ma'am."

"Are you a cowboy, by chance?" the first girl asked.

"Yes, ma'am, I am."

"I didn't know they really existed."

"Well, it's not like in a Western movie or anything," I explained. "But there are still lots of ranches, and even now there are more cattle in Texas than people."

The girls glanced at each other once again, sharing their excitement.

"Listen, Tex," the first of the girls said. "I can't hire you, but I tell you what. I know we need help, and I don't want to lose you, either. Don't go anywhere until you apply here. We have an empty room where we place our resident waiters. Usually two to a room. But one of our rooms is empty. I will stick my neck out and let you spend the night there. Then I'll introduce you to our manager in the morning. Does that sound agreeable? Minimally, you have a free place to stay for the evening. Don't you dare tell a soul, or my job is on the line."

"Sure," I answered happily.

"What's your name, cowboy?" the other of the girls asked.

"Jericho."

"I'm Pauline," the first of the girls said, holding out her hand to shake mine.

I took her hand and kissed it instead, just for show, corny as it was.

It worked. She blushed.

"I'm Margaret," the other girl said as she held out her hand to be kissed, not to shake.

"Let me get my belongings," I said after that hand received its due. "It'll just take a second."

I retrieved everything and returned to the check-in desk. Pauline was standing in front of it now to escort me, leaving Margaret to mind things until she returned.

"What's that with you, Tex?" Pauline asked as she walked with me to my quarters. "A guitar? You're a singing cowboy, are you now? Blimey."

Pauline was midsized, with slightly olive skin. I took that to mean she wasn't pure Anglo-Saxon. I wondered if she was Jewish, by chance, but I didn't want to get too personal.

She chatted amiably, bubbly in her conversation, as she walked me down a hallway to the back, through the kitchen area, on through the now empty dining room, and out of the hotel. Just outside the main part of the hotel was a long two-story building that, according to Pauline, was the living quarters for the staff. Not management-level staff, but lower-level staff such as dishwashers, food service, waiters, and receptionists such as herself. Inside the white stucco building, we went up the stairway to the second floor. A few doors down from the stairwell was the small room where I would be staying for the night. It had two single-width beds and two desks.

"I hope you're comfy for the night," she said as she left me to myself at the bedroom entrance. "If you need anything, I'll be off work at midnight. Mine and Margaret's room is at the end of this hallway, on the right. Don't be shy; I'm not, if you can't tell. *Ciao*."

Somehow this still seemed all too easy. I had little money, but everything just kept clicking right into place. Was there such a thing as fate? As in supposed-to-be? Some yellow brick road, so to speak?

In spite of everything, I was nervous the next morning as Pauline showed me to the hotel. There was a confidence inside me by now with all the assurances, but this was the real test. Did they have work for me, and would they hire me?

I followed Pauline to a girl behind the counter, where she left me after a brief explanation to the counter girl. The counter girl was short, of serious demeanor, and with long curly hair. She barely smiled while staring at me for a moment.

"I can let you talk to our manager," she finally said. "Come on around the counter here. His office is at the back. I'll take you."

"Thank you," I said as I walked to the end of the counter.

"Excuse me, sir," the receptionist said to a middle-aged man behind the desk in the office. He looked to be in his thirties and wore a dress shirt with a tie, slacks, but no suit jacket. He looked up at the receptionist, then glanced at me even as he did so. "This gentleman would like to know if we have an opening for a waiter in our restaurant."

The manager's eyes brightened, and a smile sprang onto his face.

"We most certainly do." He got up to walk over to me, holding out his hand. "Are you from these parts?"

"I'm American, sir."

"American, aha. Do you have a residence visa?"

"No, I don't."

"I take it you have a passport."

"Yes, sir, I do."

"Well, that will do. Give it to me, and we'll work on your visa. But we would be glad to have you."

A smile exploded on my face.

"What part of America are you from, might I ask?"

"Texas."

"Texas, now. Wonderful! I've never met anyone from there. By your dress, are you a cowboy, by chance? Or is that just in the movies and tourist magazines?"

"No, I'm a cowboy."

"Splendid. That will be a treat for us. When can you start?"

"Right now."

"Splendid. Splendid. We're glad to have you. What's your name, by the way?"

"Jericho."

"Jericho. Doesn't sound Texan. Nice name,

though. It's wonderful to have you. We're short staffed. We'll put you straight to work, then. I'll let Lisa show you around."

Lisa led me to the dining room. Breakfast had been served and eaten, and the waiters were changing the tablecloths and vacuuming the carpet.

"Mr. Silveri," Lisa said to a short, olive-skinned man with black wavy hair. His brown tuxedo made him look rather distinguished. He glanced up from a table that held a ledger and piles of receipts. "Mr. Silveri," she repeated. "This is Jericho, and he's from America. From Texas. He's just been hired by management to work in our restaurant."

Mr. Silveri sat upright upon hearing this, then stood up and walked over to greet me and shake my hand.

"Jericho from Texas," he said with a bright smile. "I'm Silveri from Italy. But I've lived here for twelve years now. I'm the restaurant manager. We're very short staffed. It's the peak season. You came at a very good time for us."

He then stared at me for a moment.

"Are you a cowboy? Long and tall and wearing jeans, but no cowboy hat, and those boots don't look like the Western movies."

"I'm a cowboy," I said, nodding my head. "Just wanted to see something different for a while and heard there's often work in the hotels in the Lakes."

"Very nice. Very nice." Mr. Silveri patted me on the back of my shoulder jubilantly. He then looked at Lisa. "Thank you, Lisa. I'll take over from here. Did you show him his room yet?"

"His belongings are already there," she replied.

"Very good. I'll show him around to the others now. I already know who will be his silver service waitress."

We walked to the other end of the vast dining hall. At a table near a large picture window was a girl folding linen napkins.

"Gail," Mr. Silveri called out. She looked up. "I have you a new commis waiter. He's from Texas. His name is Jericho."

There she was. A goddess wearing the restaurant waitress attire of pressed white linen blouse matched with a black polyester skirt. She had long and flowing blonde hair and eased into an ever-so-slight smile of greeting while oozing a dignified charm. Her penetrating eyes were the shade of a deep blue lake. My own personal Dolores Hart, right in front of me. Was that why I was melting?

"It's nice to have you," she said while holding out her hand. "I'm Gail. I'll be working with you. Have you ever waited tables before?"

Her accent was the softest and most seductive British accent yet.

"No, ma'am," I replied, returning her handshake.

I did it. I spoke to her.

"Doesn't matter. You'll be my commis waiter. That's entry level. You'll assist me at tables. We'll serve from silver trays with silverware made of real silver. We'll need to get you a uniform. I hope we have one your size. Black shoes, black slacks, a white T-shirt, and a pressed white linen jacket."

Gail took me to a laundry room on the second floor, right next to what they called the stillroom, where food for room service was prepared. The workers there found shoes and clothes my size, while Gail left me and returned to her duties in the restaurant.

"Meet me back in the restaurant in an hour," she said as she left.

I brought my uniform clothing to my room and took a quick shower in the community showers on the first floor, one for men, one for women. I felt refreshed and confident. Any worry I had about waiting tables with silver trays was calmed just thinking of working with Gail.

But if there was a blip in my otherwise smooth road up until now, it was waiting tables with silver trays. It wasn't like a greasy spoon restaurant back home, where you smile, take orders, and deliver the goods. Silver service at a luxury hotel restaurant meant you had to be exquisite, mannerly, and with exaggerated politeness. Gail took the orders and helped with the serving, but when I spoke I had to speak very slowly and calmly. I had to bend to serve without slumping, balance steaming hot silver trays in one hand while holding them with thick linen towels to keep from scalding myself. Then I had to delicately scoop the food, using sterling silver utensils, with my other hand. I used the word "scoop," but the trick was to use a large silver spoon and fork more like fancy chopsticks. I had not a clue why scooping looked clumsy to anyone, but fancy serving was the trick, no matter what I thought. Pinch the food items, don't scoop them. Meat slices were easy to serve, but green peas and sliced carrots were a torture. I couldn't do it without spilling some. Or to keep from spilling I had to manipulate one piece of vegetable at a time. There had to be something not easy in my new destiny, and now I knew what that was.

"Would you like gravy on your lamb, ma'am?" I asked an elderly gray-haired lady.

She looked up at me in amazement.

"My dear," she gasped, "where are you from, young man? What's that accent? It's American, I think. Is that right? Are you American?"

"Yes, ma'am."

"What part of America?" her husband next to her asked.

"Texas, sir."

"Texas. That's smashing. A Texan here serving us. Remarkable. Are you a cowboy, or is that only in the movies?"

"Yes, sir, I'm a cowboy."

"Smashing," he repeated. "Jolly good."

That was the one thing that saved me. I was from Texas, and everyone made a big deal out of it. I could spill vegetables onto the table all day, even sometimes onto their laps, and it didn't matter, except to Gail. They loved it that a Texas cowboy was serving them. I would have told them alligator-wrestling stories if necessary, but it didn't matter. Just me being from Texas was all they needed, and the more "y'all"s I threw their way, the bigger the tips got. I got sick of hearing the same questions about me being from Texas, and giving the same answers, but it kept me from getting fired, which I was sure would have happened otherwise, due to my clumsiness.

Gail wasn't happy with my poor performance; I could feel it. We split the tips between us, and I got her more tips than she ever got on her own, so she told me. Since I was new, she seemed in a wait-and-see mode about me as we cleaned up after the meal. She told me when to be in for the evening meal, then left me to myself. Her demeanor and tone of voice wasn't cold, but it was chillingly neutral and impersonal.

"Hey, Tex," Pauline greeted me from the reception counter as I walked through the lobby after cleanup in the restaurant was finished. She wasn't working but was talking to Lisa as I walked by on the way to the boat dock nearby for a stroll by the lake. "I hear you got hired. How was it?"

I nodded my head and replied, "It was okay."

"That's great."

She looked at Lisa quickly.

"I'll see you, love," she said to Lisa before giving her a kiss on the cheek. "Let me show our resident cowboy around."

She looked at me and said, "Wait up. I'll tag along, if you don't mind. I can see you need a companion."

She walked around the counter to me.

"Do you need to go to your room to change?" she asked as we walked out of the hotel.

"Naw," I replied. "I put my commis waiter's jacket in to be washed. I just want to walk around and get my bearings before I go in and take a nap or something, and then shower."

"Grand. I'll walk with you. Let's go feed the ducks. They're cute."

She led me to the boat dock, which is where I was headed anyway. And lo and behold, there indeed was a flock of mallard ducks as well as some swans near the pier. Also floating in the water were some residual food pieces that the ducks pecked at without seeming overly hungry.

Pauline opened her purse and pulled out a wad of bread crusts.

"Here," she said, handing some to me. "The kitchen saves some of these every day so I can feed them to the ducks."

She tore some of the crusts into pieces and threw them into the water, where the ducks made frantic splashes to get their share. The swans gracefully paddled over to get some for themselves, but were too late, which I later discovered was habitual with them.

"Now that they're all bloated and full," Pauline said with a giggle after a few minutes of feeding, "here's the fun part."

She pulled out a couple more bread crusts to hand to me.

"If you throw in the entire crust," she said as she pulled one out also for herself, "and throw it whole into the water, watch what happens. They had their fun; now it's my turn."

She threw in a crust and again the ducks paddled furiously to retrieve it. But since this was a piece long and thick, no one duck could take control of it. Two, three, even four ducks at a time fought over the crust. They jerked and pulled and splashed, until one managed to get the whole piece, then paddled ferociously away to protect it.

Seeing how the swans were always left out, I threw a crust directly in front of one. The swan watched the bread hit the water, then with the most peaceful and calm demeanor, slowly lowered its long neck to fetch it. By then, however, the entire flock of ducks had paddled there to fight over the crust. The swan watched in shocked amazement, as if feeling left out. Again I tried, with another crust, and the same thing happened. There was some moral lesson to be learned from this, I decided.

"Come on, Tex," Pauline said, pulling at my arm. "Let's go get a pint of bitter at the tavern. The Pub On Windermere is next door to The Old Britannia. I need to indoctrinate you to our lifestyle, and here's the place to start."

This was my first English pub. The sign over it, as we entered, had the tavern name and a bragging reference to the author Charles Dickens socializing there. A nice way to start assimilating, I thought.

"And you wear the scars like badges of honor," I ended my alligator fable to Pauline and the other girls who had soon joined our table, Margaret and Lisa. They were flocked around me at our corner table at the back of the pub. "They're a source of pride."

"Show us a scar then," Margaret mocked, as if I were bluffing.

I unlashed and pulled off my combat boot, then took off my sock while pointing to the long, crooked scar on the instep of my right foot.

Each studied it, then looked up at me.

"You expect us to believe that was from wrestling a bloody alligator?" Pauline scoffed.

They kept staring and waiting for my answer.

"Actually, it's from when I brought down a wild boar with a pocket knife. But that's a different story."

They howled in laughter and took another sip of their beer.

"Coming on like a Davy Crockett here," Lisa said. It was the first time I saw her smile.

"But he's fun," Pauline said. "I haven't had so

much fun. I don't care if it's true or not."

"Tell us another whopper, Tex," Margaret cajoled.

"I can't now. I need a nap, and then I've got to go to work. Gail's down on me because I'm incompetent."

"Gail's your silver service waitress?" Lisa asked. "She's a strange one. I don't mean that badly. She's very classy. It's like she doesn't belong here."

"Wait a minute, love." Margaret scowled. "You're saying we're not classy? How dare you say that to us."

"Gail is strange," Pauline seconded. "I don't know if it's class or not, though. She's so serious all the time. Barely talks. Lives in her own world."

"I adore her," Lisa said. "She does talk. But she usually has something worth saying when she does."

"Say," Margaret sneered. "And we don't?"

"Of course not," Pauline replied. "That's why we have so much fun."

They then raised their beer mugs in a toast to themselves while beckoning me to join.

"To us," Pauline bellowed. "And our new mate from Texas. Now we're sillier than ever."

We chugged it down with all three girls topping off the toast by giving me a kiss on the lips, one glorious sex kitten at a time—a great way to end my introduction to the social life of the Lake District of England.

I was hoping the fun I had with the girls earlier would have me relaxed by the time I got to the dining room to wait tables for supper, what they called dinner, at this fancy restaurant. But I was tense as I entered, still pulling on my newly cleaned and pressed commis waiter's jacket. Gail greeted me politely but said little and remained aloof. Maybe that was her style, but I wasn't sure the aloofness wasn't because of my previous spastic debut as a waiter.

Why can't we just scoop the mashed potatoes and other veggies with our serving spoons like normal human beings, I whined to myself yet again as I clumsily tried maneuvering the food with my large spoon and fork. Gail seemingly tried not to see me struggle. I felt like a zero.

"Where are you from?" a middle-aged patron asked me. He seemed calm and relaxed, as if a commoner like me, in spite of his required attire of suit and tie. He wasn't stiff and overly polite like most of the customers, and spoke with a loose and fluid flow of speech and with an accent that sounded British but different.

"Texas."

"Texas. I knew it had to be from a place like that. But I couldn't believe it. What brings you to these parts?"

"I just wanted to get out and see something of the world," I replied.

"Very good. I like that. Adventure it a bit. Where all have you been?"

"This is my first stop. I came from Texas, landed in Luxembourg from New York, and headed straight for here. A friend back home recommended the Lake District."

"That's just wonderful," the lavishly dressed brown-haired lady sitting next to him said. "You can write a book about it all someday. Like Pearl Buck."

"Well, we're from Perth, Australia," the man added. "We have a cattle station there. A bit like Texas, I suspect." I looked at them quizzically. "You would call it a ranch, I think, in Texas," the man said as if to answer the question I didn't get around to asking.

I nodded.

"I grew up on one," I replied.

"Perfect," the man said. "It's like we're mates then. Let me write down my address for you so you can come see us if you ever make it that far. We would love to hear all your adventures you've accumulated by then. When we pay the bill, we'll borrow your pen and write our address down on a receipt form or something."

Gail glanced over at them and smiled approvingly. Maybe she was impressed.

"I'd love that," I said. "I hope I have some stories by then. I'd love to see Australia."

"We'd love to show you," the man said. "And there's lots of sheilas down in Oz that would love to meet a big, strong Texan like you."

I looked quizzically at him once again.

"He doesn't know what a sheila is," his wife explained to her husband before looking back at me. "A sheila is our cute little slang for an Australian lass. A girl, you see."

"I almost immigrated there," I replied.

Gail looked at me as surprised as the Australian couple.

"So why didn't you then?" the man asked.

"I was in the Marines. I had to decide if I wanted to reenlist or not. I thought about what I wanted to do if I didn't reenlist. I was in Vietnam, and Australia wasn't all that far, and y'all speak English and opened up a continent like we did. You're sort of pioneers like us. I know that we aren't a part of the British Empire anymore, but we're still not so far removed historically and culturally.

"Anyway, the thought appealed to me. So I wrote some department in Australia to find out about immigrating and was given a form to fill out. Y'all had a land tenement policy until just last year, 1972. The Australian office I dealt with was excited at the prospect of getting a farm boy from Texas to come farm. It would almost be like homesteading—but then the land tenement policy ended before I got out of the Marines. The thought still appeals to me. We'll see what I can manage without the farm tenement system."

"For sure," the woman said. "Don't let that stop you. Come anyway."

"So next, I wrote to the state of Alaska. They're a pioneering state even now. I've read that a person could even homestead there. I couldn't believe it. Just like in the old days, in the Midwest in America in the nineteenth century."

"Sounds divine." The woman sighed. "Why didn't you do it?"

"Because just as I was ready to get out of the Marines and give it a shot, they wrote me that they had land dispute issues with the Indians and Eskimos there. Everything had to be settled first before they could continue the policy."

"A day late and a dollar short, as they say in America," the man said with a chuckle.

"So," I explained further, "travel and adventure instead. And here I am."

The smile on Gail's face remained as she served them both coffee. I hoped maybe I was worth having around, to her.

"The tips were good again," she said to me as we

replaced the napkins and tablecloths after the meal. "You charm the customers and have a way with people. You even have charisma. But you're still bad about spilling vegetables. I don't suppose there's hope for you in that regard."

She didn't seem angry about it as she talked. Our hands touched as we grabbed for the same napkin at the same time. A warm hormonal surge went through my body. I liked it.

She looked at me intensely, letting me hope she felt the same thrill as I did.

Dropping the napkin she held, she sat down at the table where we were setting up.

"Look," she said in a businesslike tone, as if instructing. "Let me show you how to serve with silverware rather than a stew ladle or whatever it is you use to throw slop in restaurants back in Texas."

She picked up a fork and a spoon and increased her scrutiny my way.

"Pretend these utensils are connected, sort of like an ice tong. You can make them like one if you hold them correctly. Watch me. Like this."

The holding end of each utensil she brought together with one hand as if hinged somehow magically. Gracefully, she spread the serving ends and then closed them again. She made it look incredibly easy, as if they were a part of her.

"Open," she said patiently, as a mother talking to her child, "close. Open. Close. It's very simple. Your fingertips are toward the middle of the utensils, while you secure the holding ends firmly with the base of your hand and your palm, then guide the utensils with your fingers. They should be horizontal. Not perfectly so. You can allow a small angle downwards and then grab the meat or veg as if they were ice cubes. We don't have food to practice with at the moment, but after we finish setting up tables, you can practice on your own, just opening and closing. You'll get the hang of it."

Her smile turned into a tantalizing, sexy, endearing grin directed my way. As if we were mates. It calmed me. I was ready to enjoy the rest of the evening.

It was if I had finally arrived.

Chapter 6

With each day I wanted to see more of the Lake District, as much of the area as I could manage. Strolls through the village of Bowness became my first objective. The place was so British. That's what I was game for now that I was getting my bearings, British things—fish-and-chips stalls, butcher shops with whole chickens and meat slabs hanging down from hooks, tea parlors, kiosks, shops, and bakeries.

Since Bowness was part of a National Trust area for tourists, it had hotel after hotel. As happy as I was with The Old Britannia, I pictured working for many of the other hotels, as well, as I walked past them. Who would I meet there? Did they use the silver service method that drove me crazy? But silver service or not, I was too happy being where I was and working with the people I worked with at The Old Britannia, so my fantasies about other hotels were only flirtatious.

Just outside the village, rolling green pastures began. Flat, chiseled rocks were used as bricks to build fences in these pastures to keep the sheep in, and whatever predators, including man, out. This charmed me to death. The sheep inside these pastures seemed the most peaceful in the world, somehow more peaceful than any sheep anywhere else.

Stone was everywhere, for the taking. Not just the pasture fences were built of this stone, but also the houses, although for those, stones of bigger size had been used, as well as more squared and smooth. The churches also were made of stone and had rich, green lawns around them, part of which were used for their cemeteries. The serenity of the gravesites made the thought of "rest in peace" almost seem plausible.

Farther up the road from the village was a hill, a rather pronounced one that required effort to reach the top, thanks to its steep incline. Being a Marine, I decided to run up it. I figured to set myself apart, to be better, in my mind, than the locals. At the top, I could see for miles around. The lake looked even more majestic from this hilltop peak. But to see beyond a few miles was impossible, for there were bigger hills that blocked the view in the distance, each manicured and emerald green.

It was becoming routine to meet the girls in the afternoon for a pint of bitter at the Pub On Windermere. As much as I enjoyed this and looked forward to it, the Britishness of it was what I liked the most. I loved British mannerisms, slang, and the dry wit I heard so much.

British pubs beat the honky-tonks and bars back home, I concluded. Since I hadn't really enjoyed honky-tonks very often, that was easy for me to decide. I didn't know if I would enjoy pubs so much either, if I lived in England very long, but for now, in my existence at the Lakes, they were fun, a great way to socialize and get to know the natives. In this case, the female natives, my friends from the hotel. I was always the only guy with Pauline, Margaret, and/or Lisa each day. They ate up my stories of rural Texas and the Marine Corps, which made me enjoy pubs all the more.

But how much more of my life would I want to just sit around imbibing beer, even with pretty lasses at my side, even in merry old England? And it became more of a "been there, done that" environment for me with each passing day.

"Where are the others?" I asked Pauline as we walked to the Pub On Windermere one day.

"They left a couple of hours ago," she replied. "They got off early and were bored. They're coming back any minute to relieve me. But don't worry, I can go on ahead. We have a backup at the desk. I'm bored meself, so I'm taking off early. We'll share a pint together, mate."

Pauline put her arm in mine as we walked out of the hotel. That was commonplace for the girls to do with me.

"Here they come now," Pauline said as she pointed. Lisa and Margaret were coming toward us from the far end of the alleyway that lay between The Old Britannia and the Pub On Windermere. She began to laugh. "Oh, my goodness," she howled in glee. "Look at the two of them, would you? Lisa and Margaret are pissed out of their minds. I hope they don't get in trouble at the hotel, but they'll probably be okay. Glad the manager is out for the day, though, and at least our backup is sober."

When Margaret and Lisa spotted me, they immediately brightened up. They were already giggly, but now their expressions were exploding with enthusiasm.

"Well, hello, hunk," Margaret said as she approached me.

She walked in front of me to block my path, then

embraced me and pulled me away from Pauline, giving me a deep kiss, which she held. Not to be outdone, Lisa maneuvered from the side, pulled my face around, and gave me an even deeper kiss, which she also held. I felt swimming in a sea of *amour*. Then, just as suddenly, they let go of me and continued on their way to the hotel, as if I had been a side show for them and now it was over. But I wallowed in the attention I'd just received. By the time I came back to earth, I noticed Pauline had walked on ahead a few feet and was crying.

"Go to hell," she said angrily. "Just go straight to the dogs."

Was it my ego that forgot about Pauline? I hadn't considered she would get hurt feelings from this. Should I have considered it? Up to now, everything about us had seemed a good time, nothing serious.

Pauline stormed off and began to run.

"Stay away from me," she spewed as she did so. "Stay away. Leave me alone."

I held back and let her walk on without me. I started to go to my room, then decided I had to work this out with her. I found her at a table by the door of the pub, sipping on a pint and still physically crying. How was I going to get out of this one?

"I'm sorry, Pauline," I said meekly. I knew apologies weren't going to work, but it was the only opening I could think of. "Pauline, we were just having fun. I didn't mean anything. Please let me spend the afternoon with you here. Y'all kiss me all the time, for fun. I thought they were just having fun again. Was I supposed to shove them away?"

She looked up at me with pleading, hurt-filled eyes, then patted the chair next to her for me to sit.

"Let me get a beer first," I said. "Do you want another one while I'm there?"

She gave a sheepish smile, her eyes still red, while shaking her head no.

"Me mug is still half full," she replied. "I'm fine. Thank you, though."

I was the only one at the bar when I walked up to order my pint. The bartender was wiping the countertop with a rag, but when I made my order, he put it down to look me square in the eyes.

"You made Pauline cry," he sneered. "She's a good friend of mine. Is this how you treat women in Texas?"

His harshness caught me by surprise, and I looked at him in blank astonishment, showing the awkwardness I felt.

"I don't want to see you anymore," he said. "I don't want the likes of you coming in here. The next time you come in here, I'm kicking your ass right back out. You got that?"

This made me feel all the more awkward. The bartender was muscular and about my size, but I had no idea what made him think he could take me. There was a defiance inside me that felt like telling him off, but my disgust for him overtook it, and I didn't want anything to do with him. I even resented how it took my focus away from Pauline.

I walked back to Pauline at her table.

"I've got to go," I said standing over her where she sat.

"Why, love?"

"I don't really have time today, but I wanted to be with you a while, since we have so much fun. But I'll see you tonight at the hotel."

"Sure, sure," she said, showing surprise.

I was tired but couldn't sleep when I tried taking my afternoon nap. The incident with the bartender gnawed at me. The more I thought about the guy, the madder I got. I didn't want trouble, and he didn't seem worth it, but the encounter with him didn't sit well with my cultural DNA, either Texan or Marine. Everything in me demanded I go to the Pub On Windermere tonight for a showdown and then never go back, if that's what I decided.

Aggression unchallenged is aggression unleashed. Fellow Texan Lyndon Baines Johnson said that. He said it as he was escalating the war in Vietnam. That should have been my cue to back off from any thought of going to the pub that night. But I had seen this bartender physically throw out other patrons. He seemed to relish it. Somehow I was new meat to him, and he was using Pauline as an excuse. This made me even angrier.

"You're upset about something," Gail surmised as we prepared linen for the tables that afternoon before supper. "You're holding back a scowl, as if you wanted to punch someone."

I looked at her and eased into a half smile, gave a nod for yes, then returned my demeanor back to the scowl.

"Yes to what?" she asked. "That you're upset, or that you want to punch someone?"

I nodded my head yes again.

She let out a chuckle.

"Talk to me. You've never got mad at anyone your entire time here. What's it about?"

I shook my head no, that I didn't want to talk about

it. She grabbed the linen from my hand to place it on the chair near her. This was her not taking no for an answer.

"The girls and I were messing around," I began as coolly as I could manage. "Margaret and Lisa were tipsy, coming from the Pub On Windermere. We flirt with each other a lot, and they each just laid one on me in the alleyway, right in front of Pauline. Pauline and I were on our way to the pub when this happened. Pauline was in a good mood until then, but the girls kissing me upset her, for some reason. None of us meant anything by it. They do it, including her, all the time with me. We're buds. Mates. But suddenly Pauline started crying and feeling left out."

"Don't be upset over Pauline," Gail advised. "She's a bit insecure. I don't mean dramatically so. She has issues is all. She gets hurt easily. She may not even have designs on you yet still needs to feel in control of things about you. It's nothing to worry about."

"Yeah, well, that's just the half. I wanted to make it up to her, but the bartender saw Pauline crying in the pub, the Pub On Windermere, after she came in, and he made an issue out of it. Suddenly he's Pauline's great protector."

"Which bartender?"

"The big one."

"Two of them are big. The manager is the biggest. His belly protrudes, but he's quite physically ept. Another one is a bartender only and is quite muscular. Quite the bully."

"That's the one," I said. "The bartender guy. He told me not to patronize the establishment anymore. And what ticks me off is I walked away, giving him a victory. I didn't want trouble, and it all caught me by surprise. Plus I was feeling guilty still about Pauline, whether I should or not. I wasn't at my best in a Marine sort of way. But I don't like backing down. I felt dumb, at the time. The guy was being a punk. A bully, like you said. But the more I think about it, the more it gets under my skin. I'm not going to take it. Walking away has its place. They even teach you that in the Marines, and in martial arts, too. But standing up to bullies has its place, too. We all have decisions to make."

"Is this the Texan in you or the Marine?"

"Yes."

"I suppose it's hard to change your spots all of a sudden," she teased. "A leopard can't change his spots, get it?"

I nodded my head that I got it, then looked away to reemphasize my frustration.

"You did good to walk away, Jericho. He's not worth it. Everyone needs to walk away. I don't go there anymore. He looks for trouble. I don't know how many he's manhandled. He likes to show off."

"Well, I'm showing him up," I said defiantly.

She looked at me with disapproval.

"I suppose I can't talk you out of it, can I?"

"After work tonight, I'm going there. Not to order anything, just sit at a table and wait for him to make his move. Someone has to stand up to a bully around here. He'll keep bullying the meeker mold, but he'll know somebody out there ain't going to take it."

"It would be nice to see someone stand up to him after all this time," she said. "I'm coming with you."

This doubled my courage.

I wanted the evening at the Pub On Windermere to

be uneventful, as if there had been no encounter earlier. So Gail and I walked into the place after waiting tables that night, very self-assured and casual, business as usual written all over us, an evening amongst friends. Pauline, Lisa, and Margaret had a table already and motioned us toward them as they saw us enter.

"We know why you're here," Lisa said solemnly. "Come, sit with us. We're for you."

"I'm so sorry this happened," Pauline apologized. "The bartender let me know after you left how he was my great protector. The cheeky bastard. I told him I need protecting from him, not you. You being my mate and all." She looked at me sheepishly. "I'm a crazy one for sure, Jericho. You three did nothing wrong this afternoon, and I get me bleeding feelings hurt for God knows what reason. And now this. Please forgive me, love."

"It's ordained or something," I replied. "An accident looking for a place to happen."

The three of them at the table raised their mugs in salute as I spoke those words.

"But listen," I instructed. "We need to sit at that table in the back. The extreme back at the wall. The one in the corner."

They looked at the back of the pub to check out where I meant.

"Just as a precaution," I explained. "Nothing's going to happen tonight. Bullies are cowards and hate having their bluff called. But sometimes that makes them even more dangerous. Even more determined to not lose face. So I can't take any chances. I don't want to worry about my backside. We'll just enjoy ourselves and pretend there's nothing going on. But if the matter's pushed, then it's better to be cornered than surrounded."

"Are you expecting a mob, my dear?" Margaret asked.

"No, but take nothing for granted," I replied. "Sitting in a corner when you anticipate a fight is standard operational procedure back home for barroom brawls."

"You would know," Lisa said approvingly.

We relaxed as we sat at the table in the back. Gail and I chose not to drink. Not just for a clear head, but we also didn't want to sponsor a thug. I felt bad for Charles Dickens, that somehow his legacy was tied to a bartender such as was the focus of our concern for the evening.

"You were so caring about my feelings," Pauline said between sips of her beer. "I'm so ashamed of myself to have caused you a guilty conscience, and now this turmoil. For all your supposed ruggedness, you're incredibly sensitive."

She looked at the other girls casually, as if to address them in particular.

"He is so courteous to us," Pauline continued her praise of me. "Fun, entertaining, but so courteous as just part of his demeanor."

"The Southern gentleman," Margaret added. "Calls us ma'am, opens the door for us. Treats us like ladies."

"It's more than that," Lisa said. "He was sympathetic to Pauline instead of belittling her. I don't know how many blokes would do that. It would be their chance to show off their manly wares and macho it up. Make fun of her in her weakness and feel big about themselves as if they're above it all. But Jericho knows who he is. He knows he's a man. It gives him options. Like courtesy and feelings and not having to back down from having them. I admire that."

Gail nodded her head in agreement.

"It's more than courtesy, for sure," she said. "Jericho oozes sensitivity, with me and with our customers. He has a real rapport with people. It's wonderful to be around. And he does more than his share of the work. More to be helpful than just to be doing his job."

I loved hearing this compliment from Gail. I hadn't known where I stood with her, but this made it more clear.

"I'm trying to believe you," I said to them with a grin. "You're just encouraging me in my hour of need, I think."

"Your situation brings out the juices," Lisa said, "but what we're saying is true. Take the compliments. You deserve them. And if they encourage you too, all the better."

The evening wore on. There were no Davy Crockett-type stories from me this time. I entered the conversation just enough to keep myself relaxed and oiled, while mostly keeping track of my environment, looking for any signs of trouble.

Just as I began to think the evening uneventful, the bartender threw down his wiping rag, dashed from behind the bar, grabbed a guy half his size by the shirt collar, dragged him along toward the door, and tossed him onto the pavement outside. The entire room got silent, eyes turned toward me, to see either my reaction or if I was going to be the next victim. Instead, the bartender returned calmly to his duties behind the bar.

Now was not the time to leave, as if nervous and afraid. So I hung around for another half hour before making my departure. The girls loyally stayed with me in support and companionship, and we all left together.

"You don't need to go back to the Pub On Windermere," Gail said the next day after serving breakfast. "It's a good place. I'll go back once they get rid of that hooligan for a bartender. They'll figure it out. They still do good business, and it's a good atmosphere, not counting him, and it's fun just thinking of drawing a brew with the ghost of Charles Dickens. But while the goon is there, come with me where I spend my socializing hours."

That night she took me to a place farther down the street from the Pub On Windermere, just a couple of blocks away. A place called the Squire's Kitchen. I had noticed this establishment on my walks through town. It caught one's eye, the way it carried the theme of the Renaissance era. The owner had long gray hair with beard to match and wore bloused trousers that ended just below the knee, like baseball pants, accompanied by elongated socks that stretched from pants' end to his feet. His shirt was buttoned to the side and had a large squared collar. The place had a stage with a minstrel, who was dressed similarly. The waitresses wore costumes from the times also—long, flowing skirts that reached to the ground, white loose smocks with long sleeves, and white head covers made of muslin net. These head covers were called a cowl and had a white band of matching material that circled the crown. Some of the waiters I worked with at The Old Britannia also patronized the place. Everyone seemed to know one another, and many hung around after closing. It was a much more peaceful feel than at the Pub On Windermere and almost made me grateful to the bully bartender there for getting me indirectly to the Squire's Kitchen, all the more because my companion was now Gail.

Even though we shared a table with our waiter friends from The Old Britannia, Gail and I focused on each other as if no one else existed. We sat across the broad table from one another and let our lonely, single pints of beer last all night. We just talked, nothing more, finally getting to know one another more fully in a personal way.

"So you've never taken a ferry on the lake?" she asked me. "You've been here two weeks now and haven't ventured?"

"I've walked around the countryside," I answered. "That's venturing."

"Yes, it is. But tomorrow is Saturday. We both have off. Let me take you to Near Sawrey. That's not far. We'll take a ferry ride from in front of The Old Britannia, and then a bus. Beatrix Potter's farm is there as part of the National Trust. She wrote the Peter Rabbit series, you know."

"I'm familiar with her stories, sure, and I've heard Wordsworth lived here too. Can we see something of his, also?"

"Another time. He's in Grasmere. That's up north in the District."

She said "another time" maybe as a distraction, but probably not, I had to believe. It gave me shivers to think of any regularity with her.

"You'll love the Lakes," she said with a smile.

"I already do."

"Not like you will. I can't believe there's not some creation story centering here amongst us. Probably some Druid group did have one, or someone preceding them. But the Lakes are the Garden of Eden if there ever was one."

I nodded agreement.

"If we have time tomorrow, we'll go all the way to Ambleside," she continued. "But on the way there is a small castle some rich industrialist built in the last century. We'll have a picnic there first. Just for laughs. And to get away. I can see spending the rest of the day there at this castle. We'll probably wait and do Ambleside another time."

"Just the two of us, you mean?" I asked to make sure I wasn't dreaming all this.

She blushed as she smiled.

"I mean exactly that."

It meant a new phase for me now, in my stay at the Lakes. And something inside was already churning that it was a new phase in my life, as well.

Chapter 7

The ferry and bus rides to Near Sawrey were enchanting, perhaps because I kept envisioning the Peter Rabbit stories. The farm of Beatrix Potter was small, or seemed so to me; maybe they didn't show all of it, only her house, a shed, and a garden. The house was basically a museum.

I enjoyed the tales of Peter Rabbit when I was small. My parents bought me an encyclopedia when I was barely able to read. It included stories like hers, but also others from *A Thousand And One Arabian Nights* and many Greek myths. It had me reading at a very young age back on our farm, even before I started school. I wanted to know these stories in these marvelous books. It made me want to do so many of the things I read in them, tall tales or not. So now here I was with Gail, linked to happy memories of my boyhood, and perhaps fulfilling some self-induced destiny from then, too.

Gail brought along a full picnic basket—British tidbits such as liverwurst, cow tongue, steak and kidney pie, as well as some apples. Not counting the apples, I never dreamed to eat such food items as these. It made me feel I really was in England. By the time we got to the northwestern shores of the lake in early afternoon, however, I was hungry enough for anything.

"The liverwurst is good," I praised as we sat on a

bench overlooking Lake Windermere in front of the small castle Gail had mentioned the previous night at the Squire's Kitchen. "I love liver and onions. That's a Southern standard. Makes sense I might like liverwurst. Especially spread on buttered bread."

"You don't seem too enthused by the cow tongue sandwich," she teased.

"I'll get to it. I have to psych up first."

"So much for the Marines."

I nodded my head defiantly. "I'll eat it."

We stared out at the calm lake. Skiing tourists on a motorboat were all that broke the tranquility. Across from us lay a beautiful hotel with an outdoor patio. Customers were having tea there while looking at the same peaceful lake and probably at the castle near where we sat.

"That's the Lake Windermere Inn," Gail informed me. "The hotel there across from us. It's on the eastern side of Lake Windermere, same as The Old Britannia but further north toward Ambleside. I applied for a job as receptionist there when I first arrived. That was last year in the late spring, just after I finished teaching. They weren't hiring except for waitresses. When I first got to the Lakes, I felt being a waitress was beneath me. I drove on to Bowness and asked at The Old Britannia next. Same result, but this time I decided I'd become a waitress rather than starve to death or go on the dole or back to the job I just left. I had to suck up some dignity. But being a waitress at a luxury hotel is not a bad thing. There's dignity in it if you so choose. And there are tips in it, too. Especially now, if your commis waiter is a charismatic Texan."

"I never dreamed of being a waiter either," I said.

"It wasn't beneath my dignity, though. Ah, maybe it was. It didn't seem attractive at first, me coming from a farm and all. Not manly enough for me, I guess."

"Not manly enough for you?"

"I don't know."

"What do you want to do with your life, Jericho?"

I thought for a moment. I felt like skipping a rock over the lake surface as a distraction while I thought, but I bit into the cow tongue sandwich instead.

"Seriously," she said. "You don't have a life's ambition?"

"I thought about taking over my daddy's farm. The work's hard. You have to want to do it. I don't like the work so much. I mean I do, but it's hard and hot. The sun bears down on you, the dust chokes you, and the hours are long. Then also, you're at the mercy of the marketplace. All that has an appeal to it, too, but you have to know you'll put up with it the rest of your life. But I felt productive working on the farm while growing up. At an early age you're out in the fields, on the tractor, or hoeing cotton... We really say 'chopping cotton.' You're at the mercy of the weather and the demand, or lack of it, for your products around the world. You feel so vulnerable to it all. Just a family against the forces. Again, all that has an appeal to it too. Challenge. I need challenge. But I'm restless. It's more than that, though. People are moving off the farms. When your entire community is farming, there's such a bond. Everybody seems your best friend. Not a competitor. You're up against the same elements as everyone else. We're all small fry and insignificant to the marketplace as individuals. Even together we're a bunch of nothings in the great big old marketplace. The neighbors work just as hard as we do. Go to the same churches, except I'm Jewish. Everyone feels a pride...out in the fields against the elements. But all that is vanishing now. It takes the wind out of my sails to think of the work alone, without the community. That may happen if I stay on the farm. Just another job, a very hard and risky one. And not a good way of life if I'm one of the few doing it someday."

"You're a romantic," she commented. "About life, I mean. I like it, though. It adds to your charm and mystique. You have a spark. You want something even if you don't know what it is yet. It's even attractive you don't know what you want. It shows you're not just following other people's leads. You really do want something. Something different, or big, but something. And you're not satisfied. Not yet anyway."

"I wouldn't want to be a waiter all my life," I continued. "I know that for sure. I don't enjoy it even now. But I like meeting people. Social interchange. That keeps me going. New places and experiences. That's why I'm happy here. Being a waiter is part of that. So I can handle it for now."

"You get off on people," she mused. "That's what I mean about you being a romantic. This restlessness in you is based on that, as well as the fantasies in your childhood you've mentioned to me in our talks today. You aren't easily satisfied, and you're looking for something real. Real to you, at least. So I can understand how you feel about your home, your farm back in Texas, the way you described it, I mean. How its real appeal to you was the feeling of community and identity. Now that's vanishing in your world, and the appeal of your life growing up is vanishing as well.

You're a people guy. That probably attracted you to the Marines. A sense of service and purpose. But you should be a rabbi or something. A college professor, maybe. War is harmful. I'm sick of war, and those that fight them."

She looked at me for emphasis, and I returned the look to show my concern for what she'd just said. One of the reasons I was traveling was to get away from being judged for things I believed in and that I had soul-searched a great deal.

"But it's good to have you in my life," she continued. "You put a new element into so many aspects for me, now that I've met you. You're pretty close to the gallant knight we grew up believing in, that I often fantasized about as England conquered the world in the name of enlightenment and subjected other races and cultures to our imperialistic ways."

"You don't think you did any good with your empire?" I asked her skeptically. "Just conquered and subjected?"

"India and China added lots more to civilization than we upstarts could ever manage. And we exploited them. There's no doubt about it."

"The world is always changing and growing and expanding," I countered. "Suddenly, there's a new power with new inventions and ideas. Inventions and ideas India and China weren't up to in spite of their glorious past. The new upstart, England, had new worlds at its feet. India for all its glory, put the widow on the funeral pyre of her husband. The British got them past that. Nothing is perfect, and you made good points against imperialism, but the British did a lot right, too. India was divided and locked in the caste system with its untouchables. Mahatma Gandhi acknowledged this. He still wanted independence, and rightly so, but his non-violence worked with the civilized British and never would have with the Nazis or a Stalin. He acknowledged that, too. He knew India was backward and divided, and that independence wasn't the answer as much as renewing India herself first."

"And we brought opium to the Chinese masses," she countered back.

"Yeah," I said in sympathy. "Yeah. Someday we'll do better, I hope. It's done now, with the consequences to pay. But even now Chairman Mao not only is letting you keep Hong Kong, but he wrecked the Chinese economy so badly he even needs the capitalist lackeys of British Hong Kong to help keep him afloat. The British did a lot right, even though a lot of what they did was imperialistically calloused, too. That's life, and everyone's got their independence now, and good luck to them. Accountability holds them responsible, too. I won't argue with you there; I'm just saying there is so much involved in life and world events. Since Vietnam, people act like we Americans did nothing right, and you bring up your country, too. We and England both did a lot right also, not just evil."

"So says the Marine from the world's super power. Good luck with that, too. But I for one am fed up with imperialism."

"America pushed England and France to give up their colonies after World War I and World War II, and we gave up our one colony voluntarily," I informed her. "So the likes of you are going to blame us for Vietnam, but in my eyes we were trying to keep imperialism at bay. So, Gail, you and I can spoil the rest of the afternoon talking about all that, but I am looking for a better way to handle things in the world I inherited, and so is my country, whether you believe it or get it or not. In the meantime, that's past tense for me. I love it here in the Lakes. To get back to your original question, what I want with my life, I don't like being a waiter, but I love it here. It seems fate somehow. How the hell did I end up here? I know the frivolous answer: a friend told me about it. But the real answer seems deeper…some cosmic plan or something?"

I looked at her but got no response.

"So, Gail, I seem like some gallant knight to you? Did I understand what you said just before we got into our save-the-world-from-imperialists debate?"

She let out a giggle as she nodded her head yes.

"You said you fantasize about gallant knights," I said to follow through. "I can't see you doing something like that. Fantasies seem too beneath you. Something the masses would do."

"Oh, Jericho, if you only knew. I fantasize all the time. My reserved manner is simply my fortress. I do prefer my somberness to one of being the life of the party, or being a groupie to a rock band. I am a serious person and glad of it. But, oh, yes, I fantasize about gallant knights. About bigger, bolder worlds. Of some Prince Charming entering my life and taking me away from the mundane. Until that happens, I prefer my life of books and ideals."

She stared me straight in the eyes suddenly.

"Do you believe in fate, Jericho? You talk often of great cosmic plans and all. Is there a plan for you, then?"

I held onto her stare with one of my own as I thought how to answer her.

"Yes, in some form," I replied. "I don't understand how it works, but I believe there's this big destiny thing. And we each have one, if we listen to it, and if we're up to it. If we don't let people talk us out of the search. But that's not the same as if I understand any of it. It's just knowing to intuitively seek. You know, like 'seek and you will find.' I know that's Christian, but it's also incredibly Jewish. There's something so strong inside, pushing me, and to ignore the great whatever— you do that at your own empty risk."

"You're so big in size," she said. "And rugged. It so shocked me to see this gentle giant aspect about you. Your sensitivity. Your intellect. How you care for people, relate to them. And you're deep, too. You think a lot. You want to know things and understand them. The 'stranger in a strange land' Jewish tradition is something you're a part of wherever you go, perhaps. So this big body of yours is just a bigger vessel, somehow, to hold more soul. You do seem to have some sort of destiny. I thought I did. I chose to come here, to find that destiny, or at least find out more about it. It wasn't just a getaway, my coming here. That's what I told everyone back in Manchester. 'I just want to get away,' I'd say. But I came here to find myself. To hear myself think. And then I meet you. And in so doing, I see how you instinctively study everyone like you study yourself. I'm not even sure you're aware of it, but that's what you do. You study every element you come in contact with. I never met anyone like you. In your capacity for that, anyway. And somehow, in whatever way, you seem like something I came to experience, speaking of cosmic paths."

"I never met anyone like you either," I said emphatically, wanting it to sound beyond returning flattery. "You have something in you I've never sensed before, a mother-earth sort of thing. Talk about deep. You're the deepest person I ever met anywhere. You're in tune with something. It attracts the hell out of me."

"So you're attracted to me, then? We're coming out with our secrets now. You find things about me attractive? That's what you're saying to me here?"

"More attractive than anyone I ever met in my life," I answered her.

She turned away as if my feelings overwhelmed her.

"Oh, Jericho. You're so blunt. I like it, but it can be hard to deal with. I was sure I would love hearing what you just said from someone someday. But it's too much."

I shrugged and turned away.

"Then what are we going to do about it, my love?" she asked. "These feelings we have for one another."

I looked out toward the lake and let out a huff of air.

"I don't know," I replied. "I guess we're finding out about that now."

Chapter 8

It was pure torture at the hotel to say good night to Gail and know that it really was good night, enacting a "see you in the morning" scenario before spending a longing, agonizing night all alone eating my heart out, so close and so far away.

But we still had the next day together.

There was a cinema in Ambleside playing a British movie that Gail wanted to see. She had a car and drove us. I didn't know any of the actors in the movie and couldn't have cared less about the story, but it was my first real date with Gail since we'd displayed our feelings for one another the day before.

She sat there so proper during the entire movie. I studied her more than I watched the movie. She so fascinated me. I remembered how Lisa and the girls first talked about her and this mystique about her.

I kept waiting for some sign that we were romantically inclined for one another, but she kept watching the movie as if we were sitting on two separate couches in someone else's living room. Occasionally she glanced at me to share a scene; otherwise, she might as well have been my kid sister. Finally, I took her hand from her lap and held it. She presented an approving smile my way as if she enjoyed the gesture, then scooted over to be closer to me. She finally put her head on my shoulder. Now I really and truly felt like an official "us."

We hadn't kissed the previous night when I left her at her bedroom door to go to sleep. I wasn't sure why. I couldn't get on to her about being a British prude when the fact was I hadn't made a move on my own until now about anything. I was worried about pushing myself on her. I wanted to win her trust, but the bland good night we'd shared the previous evening had developed into uncertainty for me after she closed the door behind her. We sure weren't rushing into things. Maybe she didn't really want to be with me in a serious way, I fretted. Maybe my longing for her dreamed everything up about our supposed feelings for one another. But now with this hand-in-hand position we shared in the cinema, I felt hers, with honest-to-goodness feelings between us.

After the movie, we went to a coffee house that served espresso and played classical music over loudspeakers. This we topped off with a wine, which got us into the evening.

Espresso, wine, and classical music had always seemed so snobbish to me, like what the high and mighty do in order to feel above mere mortals. But this was her world. And this was Europe. This was the Lakes of England. Somehow it all fit, with Gail as my guide. I adored being with her and a part of it all. Instead of snobbish, it seemed the world where I now belonged.

"So Lady Chatterly fell so hopelessly in love," Gail explained to me as I sat enthralled, sipping on a Bordeaux across from her. "D. H. Lawrence was a master story teller, Jericho. You must read him."

As I listened to her, I could picture reading this

book. In fact, I now wanted to read it. This book and author were further examples of the world I had felt estranged from until now.

"She is so sick of the phony and empty shells of her writer husband's intellectual friends," Gail continued to explain. "She wants something earthy and real in her life with him. Her husband simply doesn't respond in the way she needs from him, as his wife. And so she falls in love with another man."

Gail took a sip of her wine and looked me in the eyes intensely. Her gaze demanded more than my attention. I could sense how I damn well better understand all she needed from me now. In the process, I thought she was going to grab my hand to hold it, as it seemed to inch its way toward mine on the table. But she caught herself and took yet another sip from her crystal goblet.

"This book was a scandal in its day," Gail explained further, "with explicit sex and language—unheard of even for the roaring twenties. I'm no prude, Jericho, but my parents provided a steady, stable home for me to grow up in, so I understand why scandal is scandal. I'm not approving of Lady Chatterly's attitude or morals. I detest, with a passion, adultery. So condemn Lady Chatterly away if you need, world, for the adultery included in the story. But I need to talk about the 'more to it than that' things in the story."

She took yet another sip of her wine, as if to let all she said have time to penetrate inside my mind.

"My parents' love and nurturing of each other and their lovechild, me," she continued, "gave me a great foundation for my life, one we all need. So hooray for morals for a foundational blueprint, and for making a scandal of those that deny love nurturing when they are dealing with family things. Yet the enticement with this particular book and setting is that England, in the roaring twenties, was still rather caught up in rigid Victorian morals. It took a chaotic aftermath to get past them, much like is happening now in our own sweet way after the sixties, I think. So there's nothing scandalous about this book these days, in our post-sixties renaissance, but in perspective of the times, the authenticity of this story is so refreshing to me. That's why I'm talking about it. I want to be stable and happy and moral, but not for prudish reasons. I need the depth and nurturing of stability, devotion, and love in my relationships. Not just moral structures but the true essence of moral purpose. Not just the shells and facades of pretense, which aren't nourishing at all."

This time she didn't bother with taking a sip of wine; she increased the intensity of her look at me, seemingly to penetrate any obstacle inside me that might deny my understanding of the full depth of her message.

"The mischief going on these days about sex, however," she said with a shrill anger in her voice, "the way it has turned into a recreational drug culture to us, including the mischief going on now with extramarital affairs, still seems wrong to my senses. Not because of rigid Victorian morality as much as how this disrespect for marriage, and even for sex itself, is undermining the love-nurture foundation we need in our families. We are the one species that enhances love in our lovemaking. Nurturing is not just for the protection and rearing of our children but for the cohesiveness it brings to the sex act itself and thus the family. The sacredness of the sex rite, Jericho! I don't want to exclude the animal chemistry in human sexuality, but I need more than the demands of ruthless procreation dictated by our genes as if I'm some machine."

I'd never heard such passion as Gail displayed in her arguments. I felt immersed in some hypnotic spell.

"These days," she went on, "this story might be but one of many stories catering to the masses with such sexuality and language. Instead, for the times in which it was written and for which it is speaking, the boldness of it comes through and is so moving to me. It's so deep and real and honest—that's the grandeur of it, those things. Lady Chatterly and her lover discover sex together, then orgasm. It changes everything about them and their lives. It turns her into a real person, so to speak. She is so in love, but of course they are both married, and it gets so complicated. I mean it seems divinely real. These days it would seem scripted. Part of a formula. I know I'm exaggerating. Some of this would be refreshing even today. But Lady Chatterly and her lover were trapped by the falsity and form of the day, the intellectualism and materialism, with staid and meaningless marriages such as people found themselves in back then. It became a life lived as if painting a picture by the numbers rather than in the natural flow of true art itself. Suddenly, full and complex life forces jerk at Lady Chatterly and her lover, and they weren't prepared for them, yet they gloriously opened up to them. They wanted the real substance of life. The affair is appalling to me, but the audacity and desperation of being so human innervates me. That theme is eternal, as far as I'm concerned. The real live substance of life has no bounds. I simply adore that. Life! I want the full essence and realness of life. I want to experience the divine of real life itself and what it has in store for us. Does that make any sense at all?"

She picked up her glass yet again but didn't drink from it. Instead she embraced the outer rim with her lips invitingly, seemingly to dare me to drool. I wanted to believe she was propositioning me. I hoped I didn't want it so much as to be dreaming.

"So, Jericho, my dear," she said with a wink, looking up from her crystal seduction. "Top that for conversation. We're not simply passing time, as you can see. We're not talking frivolously about having read any good books lately, or does it look like rain. Lay it on me, if you have the audacity to do so. Tantalize me with whatever fucking books you've read lately. Are you game, love?"

I smirked in humor and thought for a moment.

"Here goes, then," I said, feeling the challenge. Indeed, hers was a hard act to follow. "I generally prefer history, politics, and biography when I read. I do read an occasional novel, however, and as it turns out, my favorite book is a novel. *All Quiet On the Western Front* by Erich Maria Remarque. Coincidentally, he wrote this story at the same time as D. H. Lawrence wrote *Lady Chatterly's Lover*. Remarque's story was set during the First World War. You probably know that already. I read it three times in high school. It's a story about the other side, in my eyes at least—a man in the German Army. I loved seeing the war and hardships from a common soldier's point of view, too. I read with awe about the enemy, an enemy with feelings and insights. And I loved the era, where the old world collided with emerging modern times."

She reached over to hold my hand.

"Bloody good start, my love," she said with a glint in her eyes.

"If you study the First World War," I explained further, "it seemed like a ridiculous accident. Many wars do, but this one in particular. It just happened, and once it did, you wondered what took it so long. Just *pop-pop-pop*. One thing after another, and overnight the world is at war. And the common soldier, patriotic and hopeful, seemed to wonder, 'Why? And what am I doing here? We want to win, we love our country, we believe in the cause, but what the hell just happened? And come to think of it, just what is the cause? Everyone's killing one another when we just want to get up in the morning and live our lives. Look at that guy across the battlefield from us, in the trenches over there. He's just like us, wanting to live his life. Can't we all just get along?'

"I'm sure soldiers wondered that before World War I, but there was a special awakening going on then. The world was more linked and more educated. It was more aware and more into democracy and being in charge of more of one's own life. The miles were conquerable, books were prevalent, and science was advancing. Why were we stuck with the old way of doing business in the same old tired world? And with old methods of fighting, too, but with horrific modern weapons that annihilated thousands at a whack. This book was so deep and so philosophical."

With that, Gail began to stroke the back of my hand with her thumb as she clutched it, as if cherishing me.

"You really are different," she swooned. "Different

from everyone. Here is this guy from the swamp, so to speak, from the jungle, ready to fight the enemy anywhere and anytime. I would have thought such people mindless until I met you. Especially in this day and age, when the times seem to insist we think this way about you, that your ilk just couldn't be anything but a goon. You should seem primitive to me, with this passion you have for such aggressive encounters. But instead, it's like reading *Lady Chatterly's Lover* to hear you talk, to hear the freshness and authenticity about you. Everyone's anti-war these days, but not you. There you are, analyzing life, every ounce of it, wanting peace and beauty just like a human but fighting when the fight is needed. Or so you believe. I find that incredibly refreshing. Honesty is always refreshing. So many knock war these days, mechanically, just like sexual affairs are old hat these days—when it was a sin, back in Lady Chatterly's day, that's when it was honest. Same as you now about war."

I could hear myself breathing. This was the most exhilarating moment of my life—sipping wine, listening to classical music, discussing literature. Supposedly prudish things, except it wasn't prudish in the least. It was honest appreciation of an old horizon that had just turned into something new for me. I was experiencing the most vivid and in-depth kind of a new horizon, one I never would have guessed possible.

"I wish Cyrus the Great could have made it here to the Lakes," I blurted out wistfully.

"What does that mean?" she asked with a laugh. "Another hero of yours? I wouldn't want him conquering the Lakes and spoiling all of this."

"The Lakes would have conquered him," I

returned, "and his whole perspective."

"Jericho," she said just above a passionate whisper, "next weekend I know where we're going. We're going to Coniston. It's near here, but on another lake. Some call it Coniston Water. We won't bother with the town on it; we're going to spend the night on one of the peaks near the water. Bring your sleeping bag. Leave the rest to me."

It was getting late, and we had to get up the next morning to begin a new work week. As we entered the hotel to retire for the night, we again faced the torture of being alone all night. To relieve this agony, we kissed good night. To have closure. But mostly to linger in promise.

"It was a beautiful day with you, Jericho," she said as she opened the door to her room. I nodded and gave a smile. "I especially liked the ending just now. You actually kissed me, and of your own initiative. It's been me that's instigated any romantic overture until now. I was beginning to wonder if you had any desire for me or if it was just me for you."

Her comment took me by surprise. I thought back, and indeed my memories concurred. I had let her make all the moves until now, except for the handholding at the movie in Ambleside.

"I have two sisters," I tried explaining. "Very good-looking ones. They attracted guys as if they were in heat. I heard from them through the years about all the stupid things guys do and the pressure girls endure. I need to be wanted. I don't need to make a girl's life miserable. I had to be sure you wanted me and I wasn't just dreaming it."

She kissed me again as a reply, but deeper than the

peck we'd shared before. A prolonged, wet, warm, meaningful kiss. Her moist lips melted me. I held her to me and kissed her all the more deeply. There is not a more glorious feeling in the world than to kiss a girl—a girl like Gail. We kept our embrace, feeling the warmth.

She was such a classy person. This weekend had been no show of hers. She was authentic. As a matter of fact, I loved the way she used that word "authentic" during our time together in the atmosphere of a coffee house, sipping espresso out of a china cup, and finishing it with a tasteful glass of wine, drunk from crystal. "Authentic" was my favorite word now.

Was Gail wealthy? From some upper crust of society? She seemed classy like that but without the snobbery. Classy like classy was supposed to be, I told myself proudly on her behalf. The kind of class you can't buy.

Her car was a mini, so she wasn't rich. She had to be a self-made classy girl, then. However she got there, classy she was, British and classy. What a glorious thought to carry back to my room with me, to have as I dozed off for the night. As much as I longed to be with her, as tantalizing and seductive as her kiss was, I at last wasn't tortured by thinking of what I wanted but couldn't have. I had her. She was mine. I wanted more, but I wallowed gloriously in what felt like an empire.

Chapter 9

"Jericho," Mr. Silveri said to me at breakfast, "can you wait on the table in the corner here? It's my table, but the woman there is staff, and I don't like her. I don't know why she chose to sit at one of my tables. I suppose she doesn't know I don't like her. She doesn't come here very often to eat. You're supposed to work a meal this weekend. I'll give you a choice of which meal to serve if you will wait her table for me now."

"I have something planned all day Saturday," I replied. "I guess I could wait tables for breakfast on Saturday, though. Otherwise I prefer Sunday to work." I wasn't sure how late Gail and I would be coming in from Coniston on Sunday, however. "Not Sunday breakfast, though," I added as an afterthought.

"Strange," Mr. Silveri said smiling. "When I told Gail she had to work a meal this weekend, she said much the same thing. Quite a coincidence."

He gave a wink and walked away.

"Good morning, ma'am," I said to the lady Mr. Silveri didn't like. She was an older woman, with gray hair and deep lines on her face. This was the first time I was to take an order. The silver service waiter always did that, Gail, in my case.

"Oh," the lady said with a bright smile. "You must be the Texan we hired."

"Yes, ma'am."

"That's very nice. I've wanted to meet you."

"Would you like coffee or tea?"

"I'll take coffee this morning. I'll have to come more often, if you are to be my waiter."

"Do you know what you want yet, or do you need more time?"

"I'll look a bit longer. You can serve me my coffee first, while I inspect the menu."

I poured the coffee, with a small portion of cream and a lump of sugar at her request.

"I'll take the kippers," she said as she placed the menu next to her plate. "With a two-minute egg to go with it."

I took her menu, wrote down her order, and walked away to place it. Gail watched me the entire time. A teasing snicker appeared on her face when she saw me look her way.

"Do you like it here, young man?" the lady asked me after my return with her order.

"I love it here. It's the most peaceful place in existence."

"That's nice to hear. I assume, of course, that you have a name."

"Jericho."

"Jericho? Like in the Bible?"

"Like in the song."

"What song is that?" she asked.

"There are several, but in particular, 'Joshua Fit the Battle of Jericho.' "

"Oh, yes. I've heard that song. A Negro spiritual, isn't it?"

"Yes, ma'am."

"May I ask how you ended up being named after

the city and not the man in that song?"

"Well, my mother loved Mahalia Jackson. She's a gospel singer back home. We're Jewish, but we're from the Bible Belt and exposed to Southern gospel. It's kind of a Jewish song anyway, you know, going by the words. I grew up listening to gospel, and it's easy to develop a taste for it. So when my mom was pregnant with me, she and my dad started digging for names— boy names, girl names. And one day on the radio came Mahalia Jackson singing 'Joshua fit the battle of Jericho, Jericho, Jericho,' and so on. It was like a chant and resonated with my mom. So she presented it to my dad, saying, 'If we have a son, I want him to be named Jericho.' He thought this quite bizarre, but she insisted. Not only that, she went out and bought the record and played it over and over. She was the mom, and she was the one pregnant, and he gave in, thinking, 'This is one of those weird things about pregnant women,' and he didn't want to upset her."

"Oh, my dear," the lady said with a chuckle. "That is the cutest, most charming story. Perfectly delightful. I wish I had a story like that about my name. Yes, I see why people talk about you. Listen, I get this meal free when I come to visit. I'm from the accounting office in Kendal, nearby. We handle several of the hotels. Anyway, I do hope you will take a tip from me. You've made the meal especially enjoyable. I'll just leave it on the table, if that's all right with you. It was so nice to meet a Texan. Such a charmer, too. Thank you very much."

This tip I didn't have to share with Gail, but I did anyway.

It seemed I spent all my spare time telling my

stories. It was fun, and I loved being the center of attention, but I did wonder what was going to happen when I ran out of them.

Except I never did.

"Where I went to college," I said to my captive audience after work hours, at the Squire's Kitchen, "was a military school. Like West Point, which is a national military academy in New York, except where I went is a Texas one, built out in the prairie. During the Civil War, there was a national referendum that every state would have a university that specializes in agriculture, engineering, and the military sciences. There would be federal support for this, but each state would basically run its own. So I went to the one Texas has. The military aspect of my alma mater is still very strong, but it used to be everyone attending the school had to be in that military. So what happened was that in Texas you had all these cowboys converge on this university out in the prairie, and they lived a military regimen. How do you suppose that worked out?"

"Somehow you're going to tell us," the owner of the Squire's Kitchen said with a laugh.

The others there laughed along with him as they, in unison, took another sip from their pints of beer.

"Most universities like this in other states were in the state capital or some other city, and the military part of the bill was voluntary. All you had to do about that aspect was show up for military class once or twice a week and occasionally have a drill. But Texas took it more seriously. We had just fought off Santa Anna, and the Comanche, and then the Yankees in the Civil War. So we had everyone in our Cadet Corps full time. We have a very militaristic appreciation in Texas. We started playing sports and set up a college band—not just any old band but a military band with drills and precision. I was in that band when I went to school. It's still military to this day. It's big and rowdy and more or less forms a life of its own. Meaning us against the world, at least on campus. We had things called deal fights, where you overturned tables in the mess hall and started using food as ammunition. We had water fights out in the Corps quadrangle, where each military outfit got trash cans of water and charged other military outfits, using the water as ammunition. By the end of the fights, somehow the band always took on the rest of the Corps."

"Sounds like Sparta," Gail said.

"Exactly," I confirmed. "That's what people called us, sometimes—'Spartans.' That and 'gladiators.' It was fun. It's why I wanted to go there."

"I thought you were supposed to study in college," one of our waiter friends commented.

"That happened sometimes," I replied. "Anyway, when the band was first formed, toward the end of the nineteenth century, there was no director, much less a school of music. There's no school of music even now. But in the early days, the students just took it upon themselves to learn the songs they were going to play."

"Very ambitious of them," the owner remarked. "Entrepreneurship, perhaps? I have a feeling, though, you're leading to something."

"The first band had thirteen students in it. There had to be a leader. Not just a military leader but for music too. So who was going to decide all this?"

"Surely not the school administration or anything organized or civilized," Gail said skeptically. "Not with cowboys on the prairie, for sure."

"Very good," I said. "Very good. I don't have to go into detail. Y'all get it. It was decided to have a brawl. What better way? The meanest and toughest would be in charge. He might not know how to play an instrument, but he would get his way and assign some music guru to handle all that stuff. So they started a brawl, and the last one standing was in charge."

They all stared at me, wondering if this was more of my Davy Crockett-type yarns.

"And so were you the commander of this band of hooligans when your day came?" the owner asked.

"No. By the time I got there, even though they still didn't have a school of music, they had a band director, an Army colonel, and they had tryouts to see who would be the drum major. Drum major, I guess you know, is the musician leading the drill. Our band by now is so big we have three drum majors."

"By tryouts, I guess you mean they brawl to see who is in charge," Gail said, as if on cue.

"These days they're chosen by the band director, this Army colonel."

"And it wasn't you?" the owner asked.

"No, but just for tradition, after the head drum major in my class was chosen, I wrestled him and threw him into a trash can, just to let him know who deserved to be." Again, I got cold, blank stares.

"This sounds like something out of the Marines," a waiter friend said. "Even considering how crazy Texas people are supposed to be."

"Oh, in the Marines it was much worse."

"Yeah, right, somehow I believe that," the owner hooted.

"In the Marines, I was the biggest guy in my platoon. I had college and did well on my tests, so they made me one of the five platoon leaders. In basic training, I had this Hawaiian drill instructor who was a black belt in karate. Here I was, big, a leader of the platoon, and from Texas, to boot. I worked on a farm back home, and also in a cotton gin, where I would stand upright eight-hundred-pound cotton bales. I worked barefooted and built up callouses so thick I could do wind sprints on gravel. Well, my DI—that stands for drill instructor—wanted to make an example of someone. We're talking about Marine Corps boot camp here. He assumed I knew no karate, which was true, I didn't. So he had a meeting and called me out. He let the platoon know he was a black belt and had combat experience in Vietnam, too. Then he added that if anybody even thought they might challenge him, to come do it now. 'Let's get this over with,' he said. No one took him up on it. So he looked at me and told me to step forward. Then he told the platoon to surround us because he and I were going to fight to the finish. He beat the total crap out of me right there in front of God and everybody. He had so many moves I felt surrounded. No one gave him flack for the entire three months of basic training."

"And you got paid for all this terror?" Gail asked.

"As a private in the Marines, you don't get paid very much. In college I had to pay them."

"Anyone want more beer?" the owner asked as he got up to refill from the keg. The entertainment was over, he insinuated. Time to get drunk.

I loved being the center of attention everywhere I went, plus it provided amusement for everyone before we dragged back to our rooms to end another workday. The best part, however, was how Gail also got off to my tales and yet as if she saw through me. As if she knew who I really was. Not just someone telling a tall tale, but someone who easily didn't fit in a crowd beyond the tall tales. And that's what I wanted from her, that she would know this about me. Because the me I liked the most was going to camp out with her in the hills nearby on Saturday.

Chapter 10

"Coniston Water is the third largest body of water in the Lake District," Gail explained as we rode the bus on the way, "going by length or volume. And it's not so far away from us, either. This is Wordsworth's domain...oh, not really, Grasmere is, but we're going close to there. Where we're going is west of Lake Windermere. But the bus route goes north first toward Grasmere, which is north of Ambleside, then more west and back south a bit to Coniston. I know that means nothing to you. We're just chatting, and I'm trying to give you some bearing."

Without knowing much of what she was talking about, I was taking it in, more for the history and details than for the geography.

"And do you know who else was in the Grasmere area?" she asked. "We're really talking beyond Grasmere, even beyond Keswick. That's just beyond the National Trust. Anyway, also from this general area, in Eaglesfield, was Fletcher Christian. You know, the mutineer from *Mutiny On the Bounty*. Isn't that amazing, all these historical people coming from within just a few miles of each other in a remote area? So as we stand amazed at all the enthralling countryside, there is history thrown in, too."

"It makes sense," I mused aloud, "that a mutineer against tyranny would come from a place like this."

"Coniston Water is very pretty," she continued, "but that's not why we're going. Not directly, anyway. This bus will get us to the town of Coniston and on to a park near the peak called Brim Fell. We'll hike up the hill from the park. It's a lovely walk. A stroll for you, perhaps, even with the guitar you brought. You'll be glad you brought it, by the way. The view will make you want to sing to me. The peak near Brim Fell is half a mile above sea level, but only a bit over two hundred feet from the base of the hill to the peak. It's at a rather steep, though manageable, incline, breathtaking, which is a pun, of sorts. We'll be tired, but not so much. It's so lovely, unimaginably lovely. With a glorious view of the lake below, this Coniston Water I spoke of."

I had brought my sleeping bag as she'd instructed, and also my Marine poncho to lay on the ground for us to sit and sleep on. The poncho was plastic and composed half a tent if need be. We could even wrap it around our sleeping bags if it rained.

Gail took care of the water and food. I was hoping for better than cow tongue this time, but I didn't really care. I was looking forward to our campout. The basics didn't matter.

The sun was bright as we began our ascent up to the summit, but the air was crisp. It was early September, and autumn was encroaching—a day just made for a hike.

Gail was all business as we climbed. I had the food she'd packed in my backpack, but she carried the utensils and a large bottle of water in hers. I let her lead, not just because she knew where she was going, but to let her go her own pace without feeling rushed. Also, I liked watching her tackle our objective, the climb. I felt something of a turn-on as I watched her struggle up the slope. Her demeanor was calm but challenged. She seemed fit and athletic, but there were traces of sweat moistening her skin as we approached the peak. I was used to hiking with guys who were always competing in some form, either through the briskness of their pace, the ease of breathing that showed lack of struggle with the climb, or from lack of perspiration. This signified they were in better form perhaps than their competitors, the guys with them. But walking with Gail was sexually innervating as she physically encountered the climb and involved herself with nature, and I found that was preferable to macho male ego.

In spite of any physical struggle from the climb, she seemed satisfied with the walk she shared with her companion. She smiled at me in celebration of our accomplishment as we laid down our gear near a large boulder that would mark our campground.

"Marvelous view, isn't it, love?" she asked as she took in the entire panorama, on all sides around us.

I joined her in admiring the scenery.

"How often have you been here?" I asked.

"I came twice last year," she replied. "To just get away. What's the use of breaking away from the rat race if I don't interact with the paradise I chose? But this is the first time I've been this year. I wanted to choose the moment." She looked at me for effect. "And the person. It's spiritual, somehow. I needed someone to share it with, this time. The thought of coming by myself again overwhelmed me with loneliness."

I nodded shyly, aware that it was me she wanted with her.

"Come." She beckoned as she walked toward the

boulder next to us. "Let's sit on our throne. We'll face the lake below."

The boulder was round and smooth, with only a slight curvature in the middle with enough room for the two of us to sit comfortably, even cuddly, as if by design.

"Not quite *The Sound of Music*," she said while looking out, "but where I want to be."

"I can't imagine any place being prettier," I commented. "I haven't seen the Alps, but I've seen the Rockies. They have bold, rugged mountains. They overwhelm you with beauty and majesty. Here, though, it's idyllic, green, quaint little rolling hills with lakes interspersed, much more peaceful. I used to want to live in the Rockies. I'd rather live here, now."

"I'm glad you like it."

We took it all in for a few minutes silently, as if absorbing it.

"Both times I was here last year," she explained, "it rained. Not hard, but showers are common. We'll need the rain cover you brought, somewhere during the night."

"My poncho?"

"Is that what you call it? Where did it get a name like that?"

"In Mexico they wear thin cotton blankets sometimes, called ponchos. Poncho is a Mexican nickname for some generic character, and maybe we gringos just used it on our own to describe something Mexican. Anyway, in the Marines we call our field raincoats ponchos from this Mexican thing that's worn for whatever reason."

"I see. So we're here now, Jericho. And on our

throne. And enthralled with the sights below. Now is the time to sing me a song, don't you think?"

I seldom sang in front of anyone and hadn't done so in quite a while. I picked up my guitar and searched for a chord. I hummed to myself a bit, then formed the G chord on the guitar. It fit. I looked at her as an introduction and began to sing my favorite Hank Williams song. I saw her mouth fly open as I sang, and hoped it wasn't from disdain, though I felt assured it wasn't. The times I did sing in front of people had let me know I had a good voice.

"That was so gripping, Jericho," she sighed afterwards. "Your voice and the song... I had no idea. I just wanted something corny and unique with someone out here, for fun. You had a guitar, you're a cowboy from Texas. Why not? This seemed the place to hear you. I was never so moved, my love."

A shy smile broke out on my face. She'd said what I wanted to hear.

"The imagery is so vivid," she said. "This lost love from his past. A haunting one. One day, suddenly, he sees her on the street and the depth of that love and pain laid his heart right at her feet. I can feel it so deeply, the way you sing it. And the melody itself just oozes the pain he feels. I want to hear it again and feel what you feel. I've never felt for anyone that way. Like that man in the song. I'm not into pain so much, but I am depth. This is depth of soul here. Somehow I've missed something in my life."

I loved singing it again and was more relaxed now. I wanted it to resonate.

"Lovely," she sighed after I finished singing again. "I never thought I'd like country music. I love this song, for sure, and the way you sing it. It seems like we're always saying something like that to each other. As though for the first time we're opening up to something because of the other. It's more than an opposites-attract thing about us. It's closer to discovering symmetry happening with us, instead, expanding the crevices we didn't know we had."

She looked at me intensely, as if deep in thought.

"Is that song going to happen to us someday, Jericho? Will some memory of 'now' haunt us someday?" She shook her head several times, all the while keeping her focus on me. "We just got here, where we are with one another, and suddenly I feel so vulnerable. Why worry about lost love when we're just now finding all these things we're experiencing with one another? But the song was so real, like my feelings for you. Suddenly, I'm scared."

"The song does that to people," I answered.

"It is so real, for sure."

"You have feelings for me?" I asked her.

She nodded yes. "I told you that already."

"You brought it up," I replied. "I like hearing it."

"That's what surprises me most of all," she said, "that I would feel for anyone like is happening about you—and the fact that it's you, this cowboy from Texas, this warrior, and a Jew, to boot. Maybe the complexity is what I like about my feelings."

I laid my guitar by my backpack. I wanted to wallow in this conversation for a while.

"How long will you stay here, Jericho? I've heard you talk with some of the customers at the restaurant about visiting them in these foreign lands they're from. What are your intentions?"

"I'll stay just as long as the hotel stays open. Then I want to go through Africa. From the top all the way down to Cape Town."

"How will you manage that?"

"I don't know. Bus, barge, train. It's the twentieth century."

"Aren't you a bit leery of getting disease, or being brutalized? Your white skin sticks out, so to speak. There are some bad elements, you know. People who would love to take you for whatever they think you have."

"Part of the adventure," I replied.

"Adventure. That's a word. To you, the world is your stage."

I shrugged my shoulders.

"Then what will you do?" she asked. "After Cape Town."

"Then what?" I mused aloud. "How am I supposed to know? Australia, I guess. But a million other things will capture my attention by the time I reach Cape Town."

"If you reach Cape Town," she said.

I grimaced at her doubts.

"Were you always so self-confident?" she asked.

"No. And? You grow. So what's the problem?"

She let out a laugh.

"I suppose you're right," she commented. "I suppose we just simply grow up. Then poof, we're in Cape Town."

"I don't know what you want from me, Gail. You asked me what I was going to do next, and I told you."

She smiled and rubbed my cheek, then leaned over to kiss it.

I returned my gaze to the lake below us, pacified again.

"I got defensive for some reason," I apologized.

"I guess from your perceived challenge to your self-confidence," she said approvingly. "I like seeing your defensiveness, though, and how you take up for yourself."

"So are you coming back to the Lakes next year?" I asked her. "What are your plans? Missing the rat race yet?"

"I don't know. It wasn't really the rat race where I was. My part of it, at least. But it did get monotonous. Humdrum. And I do love it here. It's a good enough living, I suppose. I never considered myself a waitress. If I do it much longer, I may be stuck doing it. I will have to make a decision someday. But for now, I'm glad I'm looking out at the lake with you."

I could not resist the situation any longer. I reached over and embraced her arm with mine. And with that gesture, suddenly the future tortured me. Who was this person, and where was I going with all of this? I didn't know what I wanted to do with my life, just as I'd told her now. That was another thing I liked about the idea of going to Cape Town. I wasn't ready to find out yet what my life really would hold, and adventure was the perfect distraction. But now, suddenly, the future mattered. And it mattered because of her. I saw her looking at me. As if I mattered to her future also.

"Are you hungry yet?" she asked me, to break the drama. "I'm not trying to rush you, but I do want to eat while we have some daylight."

"What are we having?" I asked, a bit nervous.

"Fish and chips. That's all. And doused in malt

vinegar just like you like it. I didn't bring much, but enough to keep us satisfied until we get back to the hotel in the morning. It's room temperature now, but still fit to eat."

By twilight, our sleeping bags were laid out and our teeth brushed. We sat again on our throne holding onto the view while we could, Gail cuddled inside my embrace as we watched the last rays of sun diminish behind the hills to our west, perpendicular to the lake. The air proved nippier by the minute, which made our closeness all the more cozy.

Dark clouds hovered overhead in the shadowy sky. Occasionally a cloud swooped down in a dramatic, majestic movement. As it did, it left moisture on our cloth sleeping bags.

"You need to put your guitar away under the poncho," Gail suggested, "by our feet, so we won't crush it in our sleep. And we better get inside our sleeping bags while we can, so we can wrap your poncho around us. We don't have to go to sleep yet. There is plenty of time to talk, still. We'll snuggle while we do."

I let Gail arrange herself before I tugged the poncho into place so no parts of our sleeping bags were exposed. Then I maneuvered the guitar to make sure it would stay both dry and undamaged by our bodies. The last thing to do was pull off my Marine combat boots and secure them inside my rainproof backpack. I then crawled inside my sleeping bag next to her.

"I wish we could see the stars," Gail said as she positioned toward me with her face just inches from mine. "I love the clouds, but I wish we could have stars too."

"I like this," I answered. "We can have the stars anytime. I prefer our cocoon together."

"Aren't you the romantic? But this is nice. Hold my hands. I feel romantic too."

"I want to make love to you, Gail."

She lay silent. I didn't think of Gail as a prude, in spite of her silence. We were both in our mid-twenties, and I assumed her experiences in life had opened her up to the renaissance the sixties had brought to our generation. Yet with her reserved nature, I wasn't sure just how much she cared about the Age of Aquarius going on around her. I just knew I was ready to find all this out, especially after the unmasking of her sensuous nature in our sharing about *Lady Chatterly's Lover* the previous weekend. Inside her reserved demeanor lurked a real woman desiring exposure, I was sure. All the signs told me I was the one she trusted with her need to release the full depth of her feminine nature.

"Is there any way?" I asked pleadingly. "If we tried, though, we might not ever get warm or dry again. But I want to make love to you, and at least you have to know it."

"I should have brought a blanket," she said in frustration. "Then we could lie on top of our sleeping gear and celebrate our oneness with the great cosmos, and afterwards snuggle back into warmth and fulfillment."

"At least we can want to make love."

"We'll look forward to next time, then," she said like a vow. "We now have a next time to look forward to. We'll come here for the sole purpose of making love."

"Then next weekend," I said excitedly. "We'll plan

for next weekend."

"Yes. And we'll bring a bottle of wine." She squeezed my hands in excitement. "It's fun to plan. Something to look forward to."

"Are we going to be able to live with ourselves until then?" I asked longingly.

"No. And the clouds tonight won't let us wait peacefully, either. They'll tease us and torture us and dare us to make love. They'll swoop down upon us, and they'll be doing it all throughout the night, swooping down, kissing us. We'd be soaked by morning if not for your poncho. Any restraint we think we can bear will be obliterated by the seduction of nature's taunts. But that's the reason I wanted to come here with you. Not just for the view but the clouds. It's like they are alive and flirting. Interacting with us. Like mischievous Greek gods. I've dreamed of spending the night here with someone like you and making love in them as they did their taunts, a real nature orgy. And now here is my chance, and alas, I came unprepared."

"Don't, Gail. Don't. I can't take it. Give me a break."

"Good, Jericho. Good. That's what I want from you and why I brought you here. I don't want you to be able to take it. I want to be wanted. I want you to die from desire of me. I've never had the full glory of uncontrolled desire. I've fantasized about it, but now it's here, and I finally get to wallow. I'm not a virgin, Jericho, but I feel like one. I don't like sex just for sex. I found that out quickly. Somehow we're made for more than that. More than just the outer garments of sensual gratification. Or at least I am. So I became a virgin again, you might say, just waiting for a moment like this in a setting like this."

"Gail, I'm serious. If we can't make love, I have to get my mind off all this. Please, have mercy."

"Okay, I'm sorry. I wasn't trying to be cruel. Just enjoying the moment…and my fantasies that I can finally share."

"What will we talk about?" I asked pleadingly. "I mean, something different—cuddly conversation, but something I can survive."

"What do you like?"

"The Beatles. We'll talk about the Beatles. They're British. I adore the Beatles."

"We're sleeping with God, and you want to talk about the Beatles?"

"Gail," I said sharply, "help me survive here."

"Okay, okay. Who is your favorite Beatle?"

"John Lennon."

"John Lennon. I can see that. If I was going to guess, I would have said John Lennon. The political Beatle. The intellectual one. The macho one. But go ahead. Tell me. Why him?"

"I was in high school when they first came to America," I reminisced. "I don't know what you call it here. High school is the last stage of living at home. Then you go to college or whatever you do next after schooling. Anyway, it was just a few months after President Kennedy was assassinated. We were still mourning inside, but finally healing. So all week long on television there was advertising about this British group going to appear on Ed Sullivan. Ed Sullivan was the prime TV show for entertainment, the ultimate. I could have cared less, though. I liked Ed Sullivan, but I wondered what the big deal was with some British group appearing. I didn't even bother to watch. But the next day some of the girls at school were making a big deal out of it. 'Did you see them?' some were saying. It seemed so dumb to me. But then the radio started playing their songs all the time, and I couldn't ignore that. Even though I didn't care about any of the songs, all the new excitement was fun. I started reading about them, but most of the articles were showbiz stuff. You couldn't really believe the hype. So they came back to America that summer, and this time I wanted to see them. The newspapers were following them wherever they went, but it was the Ed Sullivan show where you really got to see them."

"The Beatles made life in England exciting again," Gail said, breaking in with her own memory. "Our empire was dead. We were nobodies now. But all of a sudden, here were the Beatles, and everyone envied us again. We ruled the waves again, but this time it was the radio waves instead of the ocean waves."

"By the time they were on TV again," I continued, "I started liking some of their songs. Not really—more like not hating their songs anymore, or as much. But I wasn't skeptical anymore about them—but that's not true either. I was. This all still seemed so dumb to me. It was like you could talk anybody into anything. But by then I didn't care anymore. That's what it was, I guess. I didn't care anymore if it was hype. Hollywood was hype. And Elvis was boring now. Why not British hype? So I watched them on TV. And it blew my mind. They had so much charisma. And their antics on stage! They'd bounce from one microphone to another. And their heads swayed and bopped so their mop tops flopped, you know. Ringo was the only one I recognized, and he was so smooth. I knew Paul was the one everyone made a fuss over, and there was one that really caught my eye, so that must be Paul. While the others were swaying and strutting, one just stood flat-footed with his knees slightly bent, macho-like. He had so much charisma, as much as all the others put together, with huge raw animal magnetism. I was enthralled. It embarrassed me to like the one all the girls did. But I decided that Paul, indeed, was the most exciting Beatle. When they finished, Ed Sullivan came out to meet them before they could leave and he called them by name as he shook each one's hand. But he called the one I thought was Paul by the name of John. I wondered how he could get it so wrong, until it hit me: Hey, that was John Lennon. And I was proud of myself. I didn't, after all, like the one all the girls were screaming over. I felt special. I liked the coolest one, and the others didn't know he was the coolest one. So, ha."

"That's cute, Jericho. That was a good story. And it got your mind off of me. So now we go to sleep. Give me a kiss."

"Oh, no, Gail. Don't even think about it. If I kiss you now, you know what the hell is going to happen. Is that what you're doing here? You're trying to lure me back to the dark side? Let's go to sleep, or we're going to end up with pneumonia."

The air was crisper now as we dozed off. We left our sleeping bags partially unzipped at the top, both for comfort and to be able to move freely, as well as breathe unhampered. But just as Gail predicted, somewhere during the night the clouds made a series of swoops down upon us, as if in ambush, leaving pockets of sensuous moisture on our faces and gear.

And hot desire in our hearts.

After another such cloud swoop, I felt Gail tugging at me.

"It's not so bad," she said. "We're not that wet. We can do this, Jericho."

"Do what?" I asked attentively, hoping she was bringing up my favorite obsession for the evening.

Instead of answering, she unzipped her sleeping bag farther and crawled out, sitting on top of it.

"If we unfold the poncho," she said, "and lie on top of the sleeping bags, we can do this and still not be wet. Or at least not soaked. At least not for a while, anyway. Come on. Get up."

With that she unfolded the poncho from on top of our sleeping bags and began to pull off her blazer.

I wasn't dreaming. This was really happening.

"You're staring at me," she scolded. "Help me, then. Help me off with my clothes, if you're going to gawk."

Now the clouds tormented. I could barely see the shadows of her body, even as white as her skin was. But the tease worked to excite me even more, while I, in turn, took off my clothes.

"Last year, I just assumed it was too wet to sleep in the open," she explained. "We'll wrap up again after we make love. Everything's all laid out for us, even the poncho. We can easily find it in the dark. We can survive a cloud swoop or two before our sleeping bags get very wet. Let's go slowly. It's such a great sensation to feel the cool, wet clouds caressing our excited and sensitive bodies. I loved the feeling of it last year when I slept naked. But now you're here, and we'll kiss and caress and wallow in the *au naturel*, as they say."

"You slept naked last year?" I asked, loving the vision of it.

"Of course. Oh, yes, of course, Jericho. I exposed my nakedness to God just for the sensation. But I got so wet I had to cover back up. All the while wanting you, this fantasy of you, even as I never dreamt you really existed. So I didn't sleep in the raw for long, for fear of getting sick, like I said. But when I first experienced the clouds I couldn't help myself. I stripped naked, wanting to make love to some pagan god, and then covered back up. That's why I came back later in the summer. I wanted more. And now I have you and more too."

The saying was tired by now, in 1973. In the sixties, the "love children" used to describe every happiness and excitement as a rush, as in the rush of sensation from a marijuana high. But no other word fit the lovemaking of that night as we responded to the warmth of each other in the darkness, amidst the frigid air and moisture of the clouds. As the clouds swooped upon us, it was a natural rush, just like the sixties foretold—the most marvelous experience of my life.

Chapter 11

"We can take the bedroom in the attic," Gail told me one night as we walked to the Squire's Kitchen after work. "We had a fling last year," she explained, concerning her and the owner of the Squire's Kitchen. "Nothing special between us or anything, but I still get special treatment from him. So I requested special treatment about us, you and me. He has a dorm-type room in the attic that he uses for friends of his sometimes. Unless he needs it, he said we could use it, to spend nights together if we choose." She looked at me for my reaction. "And we so choose, yes?"

I grinned from ear to ear and nodded yes.

Our first home, and we didn't even have to move in. We still had our rooms at The Old Britannia, but now we had the luxury of a place together on the side. Alone. And all that it implied.

Now that we had our attic home together, a repeat of Coniston didn't seem as pressing. There were other parts of the Lakes Gail wanted to see firsthand with me, as well.

"I've only been to the bar once," Gail explained as she drove us to the Lake Windermere Inn, on the eastern shore of Lake Windermere and toward the north, near Ambleside. "Just to check the place out at all. I told you how this is the first place I wanted to work. It's very charming there. So in between our weekend excursions to the peak at Brim Fell for campouts, let's spend an *ephemeral* weekend in luxury. If we split the bill, it will only partially bankrupt us, but with the tips you get us, we deserve to treat ourselves this once, don't you think? I want to do it all there. For just one night. An overnight stay in a room, with a first class meal in their restaurant, and a cocktail in their bar afterwards. The restaurant has an outdoor area overlooking the lake. You can see the castle where we made our first official overtures of affection. That alone is romantic, don't you think?"

"Is this our honeymoon?" I asked.

"I don't know, is it?" she asked.

"We can make it one, even for a weekend."

She made a pronounced nod of approval at the thought.

It was a small hotel, but very clean and luxurious. Except for being in the middle of nowhere, I had certain regrets we didn't work there.

Our room was spotless, pristinely so. This hotel made every effort to distinguish itself from the rest; it was the perfect setting for our proclaimed honeymoon.

Gail and I had a change of clothes each in the one bag she'd provided for us to share. We threw them on the bed and headed for the restaurant, where they were serving lunch.

The head waiter was a gray-haired, distinguished-looking man, our waiter for the meal. He spoke like an English butler might in a movie.

"If you're not sure of what you want," he said in a suggestive way in response to our empty looks at the menu, "might I recommend the grouse. It's freshly killed from nearby. It's very tender."

Gail and I looked at each other inquisitively, then gave a nod.

"Sounds perfect," she said with a smile.

"Do you mind if I ask where you're from, sir?" he asked me. "I can tell the lady here is from northern England, going by her accent and how refined it is. But you sound as if you are from America, the South, in fact. We seldom get anyone here from your part of the world, if indeed that is where you're from?"

"I'm from Texas," I affirmed.

"Texas," he said easing into a smile. "Wonderful. What brings you here, might I ask?"

"I just got out of the Marines. I wanted to see some of the world."

"Were you in Vietnam, by chance?"

"Yeah. Yeah, I was. Now I want to see something else of the world."

"Where are you off to next?" he asked. "Or will we be honored to have you living amongst us now here in the Lakes? Are you two a couple?"

"Yes, we are," I answered proudly, "but we're not married, if that's what you mean. I would love to live here. I'm thinking of it, in fact."

"Marvelous. I was born in India, myself. As part of the raj. We had to leave in 1947. They had this idea about independence or something. Perhaps you've heard of that. Seems your country had similar notions once."

I chuckled.

"I'll deliver your order," he said with a nod, looking first at me, then Gail. "It was a pleasure meeting the both of you."

"He's a bigger charmer than you, Jericho," she said

approvingly.

"Yeah. My God. He's great. And born in India during the raj era. Wow. This completes things for me in England. Now I've seen it all. Except Liverpool. Or the queen."

"Liverpool?" she quizzed. "Oh, you mean the Beatles? Is that why? Do we need to spend a weekend in Liverpool, darling?"

She called me darling. I loved it, and not just the word but her suaveness of delivery, too.

"Yeah," I replied. "We'll spend another weekend in Coniston, Brim Fell and peak, you know. Then let's go to Liverpool. As soon as we get an entire weekend off, anyway. I want to see the Cavern and everything."

"My word, Jericho, you certainly are a fan. You know about the Cavern, where they got their start in Liverpool. My goodness! Liverpool is not so far. I mean, it is a bit of a drive, but not so much. Not so inconvenient. Still, we'll have to arrange."

"And is it far to New Ross, Ireland?" I asked. "That's where the Kennedys were from. I want to go there, too."

"We couldn't do that in a weekend, Jericho. Not without rushing it, anyway. Maybe after the hotel closes for the winter we can spend a worthy amount of time there."

After lunch we went outside to take our coffee. The sun shone brilliantly. England's last days of summer, which felt like autumn to my South Texas bones.

"There's the castle," Gail said, pointing directly across the lake from us, "where we made our feelings known for the first time. Nice to revisit an endearment, isn't it?"

"Yes, it is," I replied. "Three weeks ago—wasn't that when we released our feelings? It seems longer than that because of all we've done since."

"And you know," she commented, "Ambleside isn't far. That's where we took in our first movie together. Our first date, I suppose you'd call it."

"They showed that little documentary on New Zealand before the movie," I reminisced. "Remember? I've always wanted to see Australia, but now I might prefer New Zealand."

"New Zealand is much more British," she noted. "The Aussies are as much like Americans as they are like us. But the Kiwi are so British, still, like in a time capsule, modern-era version. It's gorgeous there. I haven't been there, but I've seen pictures and heard stories. It has everything—mountains that challenge the Alps and beaches like from a tropical paradise."

"You make me want to go even more." I sighed. "I can hardly wait to travel and see it all."

There was silence while we stared at the castle as if taking it in. But the silence seemed awkward, with my mention of leaving for more adventure spoiling some of the tranquility of the view.

"Would you consider taking me with you?" she asked, breaking the silence.

"Through Africa? Or do you mean New Zealand?"

"I'd make a go of Africa when you leave the Lakes," she answered.

"See if you feel that way in November," I replied. "Maybe we could find work in Johannesburg. We won't have much money left by then. There's a large Jewish community there. I'm thinking we could find something."

"With all the gold and diamonds in South Africa, I'm sure there must be a lot of Jews there," she said with a chuckle. "I don't mean anything bad when I say that, love."

"We're making plans all of a sudden," I commented. "What does that mean?"

"It means I don't want to say goodbye to you," she replied. "And suddenly, adventure has an allure, too."

I wanted that. I wanted her to go with me to these places. Beginning with Africa. It gave our stay at the Lake Windermere Inn even more of a honeymoon feel.

In spite of new ideas about Liverpool, we still wanted to experience Coniston Water again, just as planned, and spend another night at the summit at Brim Fell. To fulfill our vow to return better prepared for our encore of love with the clouds there. With autumn upon us, now was the time; soon it would be too cold.

Though the summit near Brim Fell was below three thousand feet, our walk up, and the view, made it seem like the top of the world to us. After we spread out our gear, we strolled hand in hand, marveling at our empire, the one we'd just conquered and claimed for ourselves, the only two people in the world.

Afterwards, we relaxed on the grass, supporting ourselves by leaning our backs against the boulder, our self-proclaimed throne.

"Have you heard of the Hindu concept of *maya*?" I asked Gail, our arms embracing while we stared out over the lake below.

"Not really," she answered.

"Everything's illusion," I explained.

"What brought this up?" she asked.

"All this," I replied. "What we're seeing now, here

on our peak, what we're feeling now as we see it, and all we feel for each other. It's the same world we live in every day, except nothing at all like our mundane day-to-day version. When I was growing up, I had this fascination with Japan and India, in particular. I don't know why. I was eight years old and living in the-middle-of-nowhere rural Texas. I don't know how I got fascinated by those two countries, but there was an allure with Hinduism and Buddhism."

"What did your rabbi think of that?"

"We didn't have one. There weren't many Jews where I was from. I was aware I was one, and we celebrated some of the holidays sometimes, amongst the handful of us. I guess my mind was left to wander, from cultural neglect, with no religious leash to contain me. But I lived in the Bible Belt. The Old Testament, what we call the Tanakh, was part of my upbringing just from being around Christians, though, so I don't know why I was fascinated by Eastern religions. I knew nothing of them, really, only vaguely if at all. Like I say, I was just eight years old. It's not that I preferred Eastern religions to my own, but it filled in some gaps."

"So, what about maya?" she asked. "Illusion."

"Everyone talks about reincarnation these days. When I first heard about reincarnation, I mean where it really got through to me what it was supposed to be about, I remembered the pull I had at an early age about India and Japan. But it turns out Judaism includes concepts of reincarnation too. Not everyone buys it, but it's there. Anyway, maybe there's something to it."

"And so maya?" she repeated.

"I love the thought that what we see is illusion. I don't mean literally illusion, but that we shouldn't take things we see too seriously as the truth, shouldn't be dogmatic about what we think we see and think we know. We have to survive as individuals and as a species and fulfill whatever it is we're here for. We have to take that seriously, to pass on our genes. But we get so caught up in that, our place in the world, and we get specialized. In economics, we say 'division of labor,' and we have our skill or trade. But socially, too, there's cultural momentum, peer pressure, fitting in. But if that's all there is in our lives, these natural, needed pressures to harmonize, it's like never leaving your hometown. It's 'life all mapped out for you' stuff. There's so much more to life than that. Even for us mere mortals. Those things are just the basics."

"You know," she broke in, "speaking of illusion, with all this Davy Crockett imagery you portray, I know you're having fun with us, and it is a good time, but you're not like that at all. I know I keep saying that, but here you are again proving it. You're this philosopher. Maybe that's what it is about you. Because this Davy Crockett stuff just doesn't fit you. Thus the illusion of it. And I know what attracts me about you now. It's this philosopher-thinker guy named Jericho. I don't have to escape to my books around you. The real you is better than a book, and your tall tales are too. The guy I'm sitting next to is so much better than both our fantasies put together. This guy I'm vibing with is special. I couldn't put my finger on it before, but it's this. You're a deep soul, inside, watching yourself live. I can see why you're caught up in thoughts of maya. You're off in the cosmos somewhere, just passing through wherever you go, as if each phase of life or place you travel is another manifestation of God."

I thought about what she said and liked it. Good, I decided. I wanted to talk more.

"There are spiders," I continued, "that weave webs that to us just look like a white, silky spider web. But certain insects see a brilliant, attractive color. It lures them. They fall for it. Next thing they know, they are caught mercilessly in that web, a web meant just to sucker them. So who has it right? Us or the insect the spider is communicating with? Or is lying to others simply part of nature's way? Is the web white or is it colorful? Who sees the web as illusion, the insect or us, or both of us? We all have a purpose in the big life game plan. We're programmed, through our genes, to fit some scheme of life as part of the whole. And I read in psychology books in college how we filter out things through our eyes, too, and our ears. We're all so specialized for survival and to fulfill some task of the whole. But then again, we shouldn't take it so seriously. Because to do so is illusion. We do have to function as humans, but we need to get some perspective about things beyond that. There's a greater perspective out there, beyond the fundamentals, and if we can harmonize with that greater perspective, great. It's all for the taking. Somehow we humans, with our minds and souls, seem to have a passport to take a better look at life beyond the specialties that bog us down. And it's up to us and our eternal search to find this beyond-illusion thing. We don't have to lose our base trying to be something we're not and don't understand. But we should at least know more about the eternal. There's something out there. Something deeper. Broader horizons. Points of reference to expand on."

"And so, my dear, you're on some quest or

something. Is that it?"

"I don't know." I shook my head for emphasis. "I don't know. I just know there's some humongous pull inside me. I never know what it wants from me. But I better listen. Even if I don't know how."

"You mentioned reincarnation," she said. "If there is such a thing, was all this meant to be? Between us, I mean. Were we destined to meet like this? Some cosmic plan? It's romantic to think. But is this all meant to be? A match-made-in-heaven thing like we all want to believe?"

"It feels like it," I surmised, "but that's just being caught in the moment too, probably. It feels good to believe it right now. It feels like I was supposed to come here to paradise and meet the deepest soul mate of my life." I looked at her for emphasis. "You. As if there is purpose and meaning in all of that. And unfinished business, too."

She nodded her head while turning her gaze once again toward the lake below.

"And unfinished business, too," she concurred.

With that pronouncement, she got up from our throne and walked to our gear on the ground nearby.

"I'm not trying to spoil the moment," she said with a smile, "but to enhance the moment. So let's prepare for tonight. I brought several towels and blankets. I want nothing to go wrong. This will be the most memorable night of our lives, if we handle it right."

I helped lay out our sleeping bags and poncho, taking orders from her as someone who had obviously spent much time planning.

"The blankets can stay folded under our sleeping bags but on top of the poncho. The towels we'll just keep in our rucksacks for when we need them. I don't want to wake up in the morning knowing we had our chance but pneumonia got the better of us. I want to make love to you tonight in all of God's glory. The clouds will be our link with God, in fact."

I was all ears. I didn't even want to form any thoughts about what she might have in mind. To even be around for one of her fantasies appealed to me, but I had the feeling this was going to be the best night of my adult life and not a fantasy at all.

"We're sleeping naked," she said straight out. "You'll have to behave yourself with any touching while we lie together, or it may turn into foreplay and we'll lose ourselves in desire. We're waiting on the clouds. If the clouds don't appear tonight, I mean the swooping ones, not the ones overhead now, then we don't make love. We still have our room at the Squire's Kitchen to fall back on for lovemaking, so we don't need to panic if nothing happens tonight. But we are going to sleep naked, caressing, but waiting. Waiting for God, when he falls to earth to be with us. We'll then lie on top of our covers and the foreplay begins then, and only then, with God in charge and massaging us through the moisture of the clouds."

I was getting aroused just listening.

We were deep asleep before the clouds made their descent upon us. Once we felt the dew-like moisture on our faces, we immediately threw back the poncho and our sleeping bags and lay absorbing the caresses on our skin of the swooping clouds' love ointments of moisture.

"Stand up, Jericho," Gail instructed me. "I want to face the clouds standing with you while we caress one another."

We got the full brunt of nature's orgy while we stood holding on to one another through the cloud swirls. It seemed like a scene from the movie *Fantasia* as clouds washed us all over, from one side and then another, in soft simulations of the water surges of the Disney animation. Goose bumps began to form on our skin, even with our embrace, as the cold moisture sprayed thoroughly upon us. Instinctively, we began to rub water streams into each other's bodies as our passion exploded. As we did so, we began to kiss. Water dripped from our hair, which only added to the erotic demands made on us. It was time to make love, and we reveled in our nakedness as we clung to each other after orgasm.

Wiping off the cold moisture from each other's bodies with the towels increased fulfillment all the more before we finally settled into the warm blankets for the night.

I felt Gail's hand on my cheek the next morning as the sun rose above an outlying hill. I felt her kiss on my lips.

"If one of us is in some far-flung corner of the world someday," she whispered, oozing with affection, "while hunger for a night like we just spent with one another tortures our memories, it will assure us, also. Last night sealed our fate, Jericho. We'll never be free from each other again."

Chapter 12

It was my birthday, and just in the nick of time my Yom Kippur fasting was complete. But this birthday was different in other ways as well, and not just because I was living the happiest days of my life in an exotic land far from home.

Gail and I woke up in our attic room at the Squire's Kitchen like we always did. We ate a quick breakfast at the hotel before waiting tables, like we always did. I read portions of the *Manchester Guardian* while doing so, like I always did. And there it was, boldly, on the front page.

"There's another war in the Middle East," I said to Gail, showing concern. "Arab armies attacked Israel from Egypt and Syria yesterday. Massively so, and seemingly took Israel by surprise. How did we miss this news last night? I know we don't ever hear the news, but how did we not even hear a rumor of something?"

"When will this ever end?" Gail sighed. "The last one was over so quickly. This one will probably be over this weekend, by the time we go to Liverpool."

I looked at her, deep in thought.

"We're not going to Liverpool," I said emphatically.

"And why not?" she asked, leering at me.

"I'm going to Israel," I exclaimed.

"What?" she bit out. Contempt spread over her

face. She started to say something, but then got up to discard her empty plate at the dish rack instead.

"I am so sick of this." I sneered as I read more in the newspaper. "I am so sick that the Jews have nowhere to go. They didn't do anything to anybody."

"They took other people's land," she said pointedly as she walked back toward me.

"And so they should be wiped off the face of the earth for it, right?"

"I'm not saying that."

"I'm glad you vote no, but the Arabs are saying it, and they're the ones that invaded Israel yesterday. The Russians are saying it by backing the Arabs. These same Russians said it in their pogroms in Czarist days, too, because the Jews were living amongst them as criminal Christ killers, even though the Jews were citizens there for centuries. The Nazis said it because the Jews were taking over the world, or whatever psychotic, paranoid evil excuse they could come up with to genocide us. The Assyrians ransacked ancient Israel. That's a loud statement. Then the Babylonians did it, and on through to the Romans. Not to mention the Inquisition and the Crusades also said it as they targeted Jews in the *diaspora* throughout history. If we were lucky, we'd only get expelled *en mass* from a country—like yours, for instance, England, in 1290, with nowhere to go. We can't even assimilate, Gail. Ask Lieutenant Dreyfuss, of the famed Dreyfuss affair, after the post-enlightenment French chose him as scapegoat for a scandal in the French Army with no other reason than he was a Jew. The Muslims said it when they took over our holy sites and put mosques there. We don't have a homeland without Israel, Gail, and we can't live as strangers in a strange land, either. So we have something called the United Nations. After the modern-day near-genocide, enough in the UN decided to let us have a strip of land the size of New Jersey, a strip of land where there were malarial swamps and desert, and where a large portion of the population was already Jewish. Even most of Jerusalem was Jewish. And now Arab armies hope to finish us off permanently. Or am I just making this all up?"

"Israel sits on more land than that," she countered. "I don't know the size of New Jersey, but beginning in 1967 Israel more than doubled the area they controlled at the country's birth."

"As colonialists or something? So this is Israel's fault somehow? Of course it is. How could it be otherwise? How could history change its mind? Everything points to Jewish blame. Again. Just a bunch of land-grabbing fools. Or whatever else you've got going lately. Gail, do you even have a clue what's going on there?"

"The Arabs feel colonized," she explained.

"They *should* feel colonized. They *were* colonized. By the Ottomans, and then by the British and French. By Muslims before that. They used to be Zoroastrians in Persia, you know. They're Muslims now, and it wasn't just by sweet, insightful persuasion. Christians and pagans used to live in Byzantium until Muslims enlightened them by the sword of Allah. Life is complicated. I understand that. But what I don't understand is why it's always our fault. I'm sick of fighting for my life in history. The creation of Israel today is the best arrangement of a sick situation that the world could contrive—at Arab expense, I've got it. But this war now is my call, so I'm going. These are my people."

I stared at her, red in the face, eyeball to eyeball, as if we were prize fighters.

"I didn't know you were so Jewish. You said you didn't even have a rabbi growing up."

"I didn't know I was so Jewish either. Until now. But I can feel it. Every drop of my blood is flowing through Jewish veins."

"I guess that settles it, then," she said stoically before walking away.

We barely spoke to one another as we waited tables at breakfast. She was cold and aloof. It made me feel more defiant.

"Sir," I said to the hotel manager after breakfast. "I read in the *Manchester Guardian* this morning that Israel was invaded by Arab armies."

He looked at me quizzically and nodded.

"Yes, that's right," he replied. "I heard about it last night on the telly. Crazy, isn't it?"

He waited for me to say more, as if wondering why I cared.

"I'm Jewish, and I feel obliged to go to Israel to help out in any way that I can."

"Is that so?"

"Yes, sir."

"Well then, when would you be leaving?"

"Hopefully in the next couple of days. I'll need my passport back from you."

"That's complicated, Jericho. It's in the hands of the authorities. We were on the verge of getting you a working visa, you understand."

"Yes, sir, I understand. How long do you think it

might be before you can get it back?"

"I'm not sure. I'll make an inquiry and let you know."

As I left the manager's office, Lisa, Pauline, and Margaret were waiting on me at the door, near the reception counter, with concerned looks on their faces.

"We heard some of what you said, Jericho," Pauline said.

"Is it true, Jericho?" Lisa asked. "Are you leaving us?"

I nodded yes.

"It seems like you just got here," Margaret commented. "Now you're leaving us."

"No it doesn't," Pauline said. "It's like he's been here forever. He's one of us now."

I felt pangs of regret for a moment from their concerns, but then defiance once again as I walked out of the hotel lobby.

Were Gail and I going to make up? Were we fighting? Was this gulf between us my fault? I was emotional. Maybe I'd said something wrong. Did she think me wrong for going to Israel, or was she just hurt about it? How was I going to handle this with her?

Gail and I ate lunch at different times. It was like she hated my guts. She gave me barely any instruction as we waited tables that night. I looked for an opening, but she was so cold to me I decided she would think me meek if I tried to reach her.

"Gail tells me you're leaving for Israel," Mr. Silveri said to me after supper as we cleaned the dining room.

"Yes, but I'll be here a few more days. My passport is with immigration. The hotel was in the process of getting me a work visa."

"I am sad to see you leave, but I wish you well. It came as a surprise."

"I know. I hate that it's happening, except that I do want badly to go. I was very happy here. I would have stayed another month or so, until whenever y'all closed down, or whatever it is you do, maybe work with a skeleton staff in the winter or whatever. Anyway, I'll probably only be here another week."

"You hurt her, Jericho," Mr. Silveri said bluntly. "Gail was trying to be brave when she told me you were leaving. But she could barely hold back the anger inside of her. She's angry from hurt, a sense of betrayal, I think. I don't know your relationship, but there must be some strong feelings inside her. I'm not trying to make you feel bad. I want to help, so I'm saying what I saw. I think the world of both of you."

"I know, Mr. Silveri. Thanks. We'll work it out."

I decided not to go to the Squire's Kitchen after work that night. I didn't know if Gail would be there or not, but even if she was, I didn't feel like explaining to anyone about what I was doing or why.

But I couldn't sleep. I lay in the dark of my hotel dorm room thinking about her while trying to doze off. I tried reading and never remembered a word of anything from those pages.

I was contemptuous when I saw her at the breakfast serving the next morning. I wasn't going to take any more of her disdain. I felt like tripping her when she walked by me as we served, food trays and all. I barely managed to be polite to the customers, and the tips reflected it. Good enough. I hoped she felt the pinch. But I needed the money to go to Israel, so I hated her even more for that, too.

It was the same for the rest of the day, but that night I decided to barge in on her at the Squire's Kitchen. I saw her bewildered look when I walked in. She immediately turned away.

The room was quiet until I sat down at the opposite end of the table from Gail.

"Beer?" the owner asked politely.

I shook my head no.

"We hear you're leaving us," one of the Squire's waitresses said.

Gail looked down at her beer mug.

I nodded yes.

One of The Old Britannia waiters there chuckled and said, "You're as talkative as usual." The others, except for Gail, laughed.

I shrugged my shoulders and smiled shyly.

"So tell us about it, bloke," the same waiter challenged.

"I'm going to Israel," I replied.

"Yes, that's what we heard," he said. "When do you leave?"

"When I get my passport back. The hotel was getting me a work visa, so it's with the authorities until they can get it back."

"What brought this on?" another Squire's waitress asked. "We know you're Jewish, but to just up and go to war? You just got back from Vietnam. Seems you'd be sick of war."

"I'm sick to death of war," I answered. "That's why I'm going."

Everyone, except for Gail, laughed yet again.

"That makes bleedin' sense," another of the waiters

from The Old Britannia said. "I think I'll go with you and get me bleedin' head blown off, since I hate war so much meself." He held up his mug as if to toast. "Cheers, mate."

"Jericho," the first of the Squire's waitresses interjected, "the Lakes and Bowness are as peaceful and grand a home as any of us have ever had. I never loved a place so much in all my life. You came into our lives this past summer and I love it even more with you in our midst. You belong here with us. You are the kindest soul I ever saw, in spite of your alligator stories and barroom brawls. There aren't enough people like you, mate. War has the power to twist souls. Stay with us, love. We adore you." She looked at Gail. "Especially Gail. I never saw her so happy. You have a gift. We don't want to lose you."

Gail flinched in embarrassment, then bobbed her head in a mocking way before taking a sip of her beer.

"Let them fight it out, mate," the first of The Old Britannia waiters said. "She's right. There are enough crazies in the world. You might get twisted. How are you going to survive emotionally if you allow two wars in your life in such a short time? It will have a detrimental effect."

"If it doesn't make sense to you," I replied, "I don't know what I can tell you to change your minds."

Gail then looked at me pointedly.

"How is your going to Israel going to change anything?" she asked coldly. "What did you accomplish in Vietnam? All those lives lost, and for what?"

"Did you lose anyone over there?" I asked pointedly, looking directly back at her. "I did. I lost relatives I never met in World War II, also, just across the Channel in France. I don't know why there's war. But mostly I don't know why I have to answer to you. If you really wanted to know, I'd love to tell you. I don't know why the likes of Stalin and Mao, or Castro and Che, or even Ho Chi Minh, ended up being so innocent to you in your mind. Or why America looks so guilty for standing up to them. I'm not at all sure we were wise to get into that war in Vietnam, but I don't feel guilty about it, as if we're the bad guy, just because the rest of my generation believes that. It's all over an economic system, somehow, except it's not that at all. Or they think it's only a civil war and none of our business. That's what they said about Cuba when Castro took over, ninety miles off our shores. Not to mention the millions of lives reeducated, including by firing squads, in these places even as they aligned with China and the Soviets, historical enemies or not. I know why the Jews thought they needed a homeland, but I also understand why the Arabs are bugged about losing that land for it. And so they invaded Israel because of it. And invaded again. And again and again. Jews got killed in the Warsaw ghetto in World War II for resisting Nazi genocide, and in Auschwitz for not being able to resist. What is it I'm not supposed to fight over? Because not fighting means peace or something? I don't show up and there's peace? Are we missing a Gandhi here or a Martin Luther King? Is that the problem? We hold hands and sing 'We Shall Overcome' and go home and imbibe another pint and feel love and smug self-gratification? In World War II, the rest of the world found the exact same reasons to let the Jews rot in the gas chambers. And here we go again. Peace, love, dope, y'all."

"The Israelis are losing, you know," the owner of the Squire's Kitchen said. "Arab troops surprised them, and the Israelis are scrambling to stop them."

"And so why go, right?" I mocked. "I might get killed over a lost cause?"

"Is this some Alamo thing in you?" Gail asked with the bite still in her tone.

"If I have to die, and I do someday anyway, this is how I want it to be, if it comes to that."

"Ahhh…" She scowled. "You're hopeless."

"You've made up your mind, then," the owner said.

I nodded yes in short, vivid jerks of my head.

"I remember how Jericho stood up to that bartender in the Pub On Windermere," the second Squire's waitress commented. "The one bloke in this entire village to stand up to that bully." She raised her mug to salute me. "I believe in you, Jericho. I don't know why there's war either, and if not going helped anything, then why go. But taking a stand is worth it. I don't know whose right in that war in the Middle East, but the Arabs invaded, and they intend to wipe Israel off the face of the earth. I may go with you."

I nodded approval, then stood up to leave.

"Wait," Gail shouted at me, vulnerability in her voice.

She got up, walked to me, and wrapped her arms around me to embrace me while burying her head on my chest.

"Don't go," she whispered. "Don't go. Don't leave me. Please stay."

She looked up at me, and we kissed. Everyone watched silently as we did so. And then we walked to the stairwell behind the kitchen to make our way to the attic. Our attic.

Chapter 13

Gail and I fought back tears as we finished the remembrances about our days together in the Lake District of England. We looked deeply into one another's eyes, sitting across from each other in her dining room, still holding onto each other's hands affectionately. Longing now filled in the missing pieces from our years spent apart, longing that came from those days.

Finally, she pursed her lips and prepared to speak.

"I got bored with my life," she reminisced in parallel with my story. "I could see meself teaching in Manchester for the rest of my days. I would have loved to have seen the world, back then when I had the chance. I should have gone to Israel with you and shooed that Israeli girl away from you from the outset. But the Lakes are so peaceful. That was enough of the world for me at the time. And I wasn't into wars, either. I had taken leave from teaching to work as a waitress in that luxury hotel on Lake Windermere, just waiting for the love of my life, who arrived like some Davy Crockett from Texas. Not quite what I had in mind."

"John Lennon said something like, 'Life is what happens while you're making other plans.' " I chuckled.

"Oh, yes, John Lennon. Your hero. We never did make it to Liverpool, to poke at a bad memory, nor to New Ross, Ireland, to show reverence to John F.

Kennedy's ancestry."

"Speaking of John Lennon," I said solemnly, "where were you when you heard about him getting shot?"

"Australia," she replied. "See what you did to me? I never could settle down after you. You lit a fire inside me, and I never could just sit and be a schoolmarm after that. So John Lennon was killed not even a year ago, and in the months before that I had been traveling around. It amazes me, now that I think about it. My traveling was related to you somehow. I was never the same after I met you. You were so full of life, and you wanted so many things, and it rubbed off on me. You had a fire inside you, a marvelous fire, and the audacity to know you didn't know anything. You didn't know answers to all the questions inside you, questions about life, but mostly about what to do with your life. I envy you that, just thinking about it now. The rest of us tried so hard to fit. That's what we're supposed to do, just fit like a cog on a turning wheel or something. But you, as it turned out, either because of the displacement inside you about the Vietnam war or because you are the most complex person I ever met anyway, knew more about yourself than all the rest of us knew about ourselves, thanks to this search inside you. You knew, unlike the rest of us, there was more to life. You just didn't have answers and couldn't live with that. The rest of us just assumed no one can know all that. Maybe your heritage as a stranger in a strange land put the fire in you for answers. But in my case, I was already restless, some, when I met you, but I never got past the Lakes as far as adventure or any life quest was concerned, at the time. Anyway, a little over a year ago I got a job offer in New

Zealand. After I quit my teaching job, I wanted to see something first along the way, so I didn't venture straight to New Zealand."

"What were you doing in New Zealand?" I asked.

"I never made it there, love. But remember that travel documentary we saw together in Ambleside, about New Zealand? Somehow that stuck with me. Especially since you made a big deal out of it. So I found a governess job in Auckland, in New Zealand. I flew to India first and decided to see the Himalayas before I settled into the job. I took a train from Delhi and made it to Nepal. How marvelous those mountains are! But it's so dirty there...the poverty, the hygiene... I got so sick. I developed a fever and had bacteria in my intestines. Not good ones, but all sorts of foul creatures. My intestines fevered and swelled so fiercely they became, like, glued together, if I understand it correctly. The full brunt didn't hit until I arrived in Australia, and I ended up in a hospital there in Perth. I was just beginning to get me health back when I heard that in New York the ex-Beatle John Lennon was murdered. Somehow that could happen only in America. But I thought of you. And here I was now, following in your footsteps, so to speak. It occurred to me the impact you made on my life. Not just our feelings for one another, one-of-a-kind feelings, but I admired so much about you. I detested the war in Vietnam, but you were real to me and not this baby killer I kept hearing such as you would be. You believed in what you were doing. The same guy that left me to devotedly defend Israel, his other homeland. You believed in these causes. It wasn't so clear cut anymore, all this anti-war sentiment I had. And suddenly, lying there in my hospital bed in Perth,

Australia, there was loss inside me about not having you in my life anymore. I grieved at our memory and the loss I felt with things being over between us. I had kicked you out of my life just three years prior; it was over that much. I had time to think things through while I was sick in the hospital. I felt so vulnerable, and in my weakness and vulnerability, it was you I needed and wanted. The only comfort I had while I lay in the hospital was your memory, your presence inside me."

"I guess all this has a purpose, so I'll limit the regrets," I answered with a sigh. "But I wish I had been there with you. And all the lost time between us pulls at me even more now."

"Yes, I so wanted you there," she said with a smile, "my knight in shining armor. And I regretted insufferably all the lost time."

"But I don't understand why people get these images of American servicemen," I said as I took a sip of tea. "You know, 'baby-killer goons' applied to us. I sort of understand, because it did happen to a certain extent, but it's like people want to believe that about us and don't bother not to believe it. They dehumanize us for the sake of winning an argument, or cause, rather than seek out the truth. Somehow the anti-war, anti-establishment cause was bigger than truth as a cause. They could feel guiltless about hating us and blaming us. That's the purpose of dehumanizing, anyway, and as a Jew I should have it down by now. Why work things out when you have an argument to win, a cause that must prevail? There is such a thing as a goon in the military, but there were so many devoted servicemen, too. And we weren't so naïve, either. Not like people say, anyway. At eighteen or twenty years old, who isn't naïve? But so were those who burned the flag. The anti-warriors made out as if we believed lies so easily, while they weren't naïve but instead so enlightened. The ones naïve were those who believed the Communists were freedom fighters. The Communists and their supporters may have seen themselves that way, as freedom fighters, but I don't know why that's not naïve, since it's pathetically naïve. Anyway, it probably was best you didn't come with me to Israel. You'd have been a distraction."

"A distraction from your girlfriend?"

"You would have questioned everything the Israelis did, Gail. As they were fighting for their lives, you would have been skeptical. With you not there, I got to focus on learning more about my people and Israel's situation and future."

"What makes you say that, love? I wouldn't have interfered with your view of Israel."

"The way you got after me when I told you I was going to Israel to help the cause, that's what makes me say that. It was as if the Israelis had started the war."

"I hate war, Jericho. I detest all this violence and insanity. I don't blame Israel; I blame everyone. Even the British Mandate caused so much of this. And the Israelis occupy so much of other people's land. They're even building settlements on occupied territory."

"And when Sadat flew to Jerusalem to make peace in 1977," I countered, "Israel gave most of that land up. I was there in Israel when Sadat landed for peace. I headed there yet again after I went to see you in Manchester and you rejected me that time. The Israelis worked all that out with Sadat and Egypt while I was there, and they would have with the Arabs in general, too, upon knowing real peace was at hand and had a chance. The Israelis gave up all the same conquered territory back in 1956, with the Suez crisis, after they took it—with nothing to show for giving it back except more war and hostility from the Arabs. And now they have given most of it up yet again. This time at least there's peace with Egypt to show for it, thank God."

"I was angry with you when you left me for Israel. It so hurt me, how you left me. And now, come to find out, you left me behind gladly, this distraction in your life, while I was never so in love—so thoroughly, in such depth in love—with someone in my whole life. And then one day, poof, he's gone. Just like that. It didn't endear war to me for the better, now, did it?"

"I understand that part," I said in sympathy. "Emotions take all kinds of turns. But it made things hard to work out about me going to Israel. Going to Israel was a major turning point in my life. I had to see it through."

She nodded her head as if to accept my overture.

"When I arrived in Tel Aviv during the war," I said, wanting to bring the focus onto why I felt obliged to go, "there were people from the Jewish Agency waiting for all the volunteers like me flying in every day. Ten thousand of us arrived per day, I heard. We were so concerned for Israel's very survival, with another holocaust at hand, for all we knew, there was an electricity in the air there binding us together. In spite of the seriousness of the circumstances, it was exciting to be a part of it all."

"Would it have swayed me, Jericho? Especially being there with you and for you? Even if I didn't feel all you did about events and Israel, maybe being there might have swayed me."

"I don't know," I answered, shaking my head. "I want to believe so. I just know I had to be there, and at the time it was the most important thing in my life. I was skeptical you would give Israel a fair view. Anyway, Gail, the Jewish Agency put us up and found us jobs. That's how I ended up on a kibbutz. And soon after I arrived, there was a temporary ceasefire. Some of the troops from the front were allowed to go home for a couple of days. These troops would hitchhike from the front lines to their homes. Israeli radio would advise listeners of this and say to be sure to pick them up if they saw them on the highway. And while I walked the beach in front of the hotel the Jewish Agency put us up in, I'd watch these soldiers who were home on leave, in their bathing suits but with their rifles slung over their shoulders, wading in the Mediterranean and holding hands with their girlfriends. Then they would hitchhike back to the front. It incredibly moved me. I can't tell you what it means to me to be a Jew. And for the first time it got through to me how much I loved being that, a Jew, in spite of the stigma, and in spite of us being portrayed as the evil in each place we went throughout history. Even today, I guess. I could never express to you the way I feel about being Jewish, the love I have for my people."

Gail pulled her hand from mine to rub my hair affectionately with her fingertips.

"You are the most sensitive person I ever met," she said. "It overwhelms me. I remember thinking this back then, in the Lakes, and us talking about it. Just as I pictured a Marine as a baby killer, I assumed this big, tall, muscular Southerner had to be a walking machismo machine. But you're everything you're not supposed to be. You have the right to feel the way you do. You're the only Vietnam vet I ever met, so I don't know how many are like you, but here the rest of us were, judging your like. And as we chastised you for being a goon in our eyes, we also chastised you to not stereotype others, which is exactly what we were doing about you. And self-righteously so, in the process. Yes, you're right, we felt we had to dehumanize you to justify how we judged you, to make an excuse for our own self-righteousness."

I leaned over and kissed her. And no matter how much I released the passion I felt inside, more came out as we kept kissing each other and I met her still ever-so-precious lips.

"Let's go shower," she said between gasps for breath. "Then make love—eternal, ecstatic, marvelous love."

Gail and I were of the sixties. Compared to much of our generation, we were old-fashioned. But the sexual-revolution facet of our youth movement scored some points with us. Parts of it felt marvelous and free to us. "Liberated" was the word used then. The pill and other contraceptives alleviated much of the angst about sex, and though we didn't accept free love to the fullest, most irresponsible extent, we happily complied with the grandeur of sex between consenting adults, namely ourselves. Stigma-free sex, but in our case, sex tempered by a need for mutual nurturing and devotion over mere sense gratification.

I had a religious nature about me, even though I seldom went to religious services. I could appreciate trying to separate ourselves, the human race, from the so-called lower animals. Sex, like anything else, could be in excess: an addictive, mindless, sensational drug; a dangerous and harmful toy to the irresponsible. While mother nature meant well with her strong-willed sexual obsessions forced down our throats, I could see she was part of some Darwinian world of survival mechanisms. Replenish the earth at all costs, and let the strong work it out. But with modern science and medicines available, the world was mercilessly more than replenished. With economic systems abundant for human life proliferation, I appreciated what my ancestors, the ancient Hebrews, devised to put some kind of perspective to the excesses mother nature seemed to demand of us, and how Jews tried to put a human face to an often violent system of genetic survival we inherited as humans. Through the centuries, that attempt at a human face toward sex too often got distorted, maybe for good reasons. Such hard disciplines and dogmas by certain religious groups may have been the best way to curtail mother nature's imperialism.

But the sexual revolution offered hope to deal with these excesses now. We now lived late in the twentieth century, with new scientific discoveries, philosophical insights, and enlightenments in our world. It felt glorious to break away into new horizons and get the most out of being human. Human sex entailed so much more than just the sex act itself. The sex act alone was complicated and strong. To flow with it even mechanically was somewhat fulfilling, compared to simply condemning it all as sin. Yet it easily left something lacking. The sex act alone—out of context, so to speak—could feel like not getting past the book cover into the full literature of sex as part of making love. We have an intellect as well as a soul to enhance our being and increase our chances of survival as a species. That is the most glorious part of sex, the depth to which this lovemaking can take us.

With Gail and me, it was a glorious mixture. Spiritual sexual bliss mixed with the allure of pure raw, animal, erotic pleasure. This seemed another cosmic element to our relationship. We had discovered sexual bliss together—similar, in some ways, to the star-crossed lovers in *Lady Chatterly's Lover*. And now, we wanted to renew our sexual harmony.

The shower together was the ultimate in foreplay. We equated it to ablutions, as in a religious rite. Each step was a ritual: the disrobing as the water awaited us, flowing from the shower; the trust and exhilaration as we took off each piece of clothing; a gentle kiss and embrace before entering the shower; sharing the warm, massaging water as we let it cleanse our bodies and soak our hair. All was done in pristine silence.

We washed each other down with soap while the fragrance of the perfumed bar relaxed us as we rubbed each other's skin, reveling in the sensuousness. We kissed again as the suds ran off our bodies from the shower stream.

The last stage, drying each other with a towel, sealed the rite. With slow, deliberate strokes, we wiped the soft, absorbent towel over each part of our hypersensitive skin.

We allowed our hair to drip its wetness, giving a feeling of primordial bliss, as if emerged from an oasis pool. Then, in bed, the cool moisture from our hair rubbed off on the pillow as we lay dwelling in embrace, the feeling of skin on skin, the warmth of impassioned bodies, and the intermingling of spirit as we kissed again and again.

But with each kiss the urges became more demanding, until finally the sex act itself took command. As we responded to each impulse, it was all we could do to keep up and to please.

At last came the glow of aftermath, ecstatic fulfillment attained as we once again lay in solemn, glorious embrace while recuperating.

"Switzerland seems so near," Gail said as if thinking aloud while we wallowed in bed in the shadows of darkness. "After all these years, to find out you are so near. Yet now, all of a sudden, it seems so far away. What will we do? The closeness is just a tease. It makes it even more frustrating in some ways. How will we manage?"

"Let's just play it out," I replied. "Answers come. The desire just wants our attention."

"We are really in love, aren't we? I feel one hundred percent woman," she said in celebration. "How wonderful to feel it. I love being a woman. Because of you. Unabashedly a woman. Your woman."

Chapter 14

The sunlight awoke us the next morning. A new day. A new life.

"I want to show you our museum, Jericho," Gail said at breakfast. "I have two paintings being displayed there. Did I ever show you my paintings?"

My mouth flew open in awe.

"I didn't know you were an artist," I said.

"Surely not. Surely I told you I painted. I'm quite good, I must say. And now, as if to prove it, I have two paintings in our museum of fine art here. I'm proud. Boastfully so. I want you to be proud of me."

"How did I not know, even with you not having mentioned it before?"

"What do you mean, love?"

"Every girlfriend I ever had was an artist of some sort."

"Oh, Jericho. Please. Please, my dear. Don't do this. Don't spoil all this. What a glorious renewal of us, what glorious sex together. Don't bring up all your women."

"No, no, Gail. That's not it. It's just spooky is all. But it makes more sense now, this attraction between us. There is something so eerie about how all this works. There's this love-at-first-sight phenomena. I see a girl and immediately I'm drawn to her. Not because she's physically attractive or super charismatic, just a hypnotic pull. And then we are drawn, like some fate, to each other. And every one has been an artist. I don't know if they've had success like paintings in a museum, but they're real artists. And now you."

"Was the Israeli an artist?"

"No, not at all. I wasn't attracted to her anyway. She came and got me. And there was a war going on. I liked her a lot, she was very good to me, but all that was more like an adventure. That's not what I'm talking about. I'm talking about this sixth-sense stuff. Oh, Gail. Excuse the dramatics, but this scares me. I don't want to be superstitious. But there's some sixth sense, I'm telling you."

"I believe you. Even though you can't paint, I believe you have this cosmic link to artistic souls somehow. Anyway, you've said it. It's interesting, but I don't want to spoil what's happening between us, speaking of cosmic links. So let me show you the museum and feel worth something again, now that I'm on the dole."

I don't get off much on art. Nor do I like poetry much, except song lyrics. So why this allure of artists? I don't know, but I let her show me the museum. All I got out of it was the joy of seeing her open up her world to me, exposing her inner eye that only artists seem to have. I loved listening to her explanations on the imagery and the shadings of each painting she showed me, the history of different facets of art, and seeing her pride as she showed me her paintings. Both exuded a haunting scene, somehow linked to this somberness about her, one in a dimly lit forest and one of a foggy lake. I didn't know what to make of them or what they exposed about her. I just knew I loved her more for it.

"You must leave tomorrow?" she asked as we walked from the museum to her car.

I nodded that I did.

"I'm glad you came, but, my word, just like that it's over. Are we going to be able to live like this?"

I shook my head no. I tried to think of something encouraging to say but couldn't.

"Should we do anything or just go home and be?" she asked in a melancholy tone.

"Let's just go home," I said.

That night, the shower seemed more sacred, but as a goodbye rather than the celebration of renewal the night before had made for us. Then we went straight to bed to make love in solemn, almost desperate overtures. As we lay in the darkness of her room afterwards, we searched for revelations of what to do with our lives in dealing with the torture of being in love.

"I know what I want, Jericho," she said. "That's the good in all of this. I'm old enough. I've seen enough. I know exactly what I want. And you know what I'm talking about. It's you. I want you. It's refreshing to know this."

"We can't afford to call every day," I said. "We can write. We'll write every day and call once a week. I'll call you."

"And let nature take its course?" she asked with a sigh.

"What else can we do?"

When the sun woke us the next morning, we made love with even more passion, as if needing a reprieve from our fate of departure and using the passion as a vow about our future. There was a need to establish our territoriality with one another.

As we got up, before going to breakfast, Gail walked to her closet to retrieve something.

"Remember this?" she asked.

My eyes lit up.

"My old guitar," I replied, smiling. "I left it when I stormed out of here four years ago. I figured out I'd left it before I was even out of Manchester, but I wasn't about to come back for it."

"You saved it for now," she said sentimentally. "Speaking of cosmic links or whatever, sing to me before you leave. We have time for a song from you. I'll never forget your sweet voice when you sang to me on the peak of Brim Fell, and in the time we lived together in the attic of the Squire's Kitchen. I was so shocked you could sing at all, but it made sense when I thought about it later. Again, you weren't the Davy Crockett one would expect, much less the baby killer, but a soft, passionate, resonant voice and soul. The voice of an artist. Sing to me, artist to artist."

I took the guitar from her. The nylon strings were old, and it took me a couple of minutes to get the guitar back in tune.

I formed the A minor chord, strummed it once, and looked up to her to explain the song I wanted to sing.

"The temple in Jerusalem was razed by the Romans on August 16, 70 AD," I began. "There was no Israel to speak of after 135 AD, and technically not since 73 AD. The last remnant of that temple still stands in the Old City of Jerusalem, on Temple Mount in the Jewish Quarter. It's called the Western Wall; some call it the Wailing Wall. It got that name after the Romans drove out the Jews, for the most part, and turned Palestine into a pagan Roman province. Jews would come to pray at the sacred spot after bribing Roman guards. And weep."

I felt myself choking up as I pictured the scene I had just described to her, and paused to get my composure. Gail instinctively reached out to comfort me, but then held back to allow me to regroup.

"For much of two thousand years, Jews had to scheme to find a way to pray at our most precious and holy site, which was ruled by everyone but us. Then, in 1967, once again facing annihilation, Israel made a bold pre-emptive strike against emerging Arab forces and recaptured Temple Square. I have pictures of it— Moshe Dayan entering and touching the sacred stones. The Arabs wouldn't allow us there while it was in their possession, but now it was ours again. Ours. Beautifully, sacredly, preciously ours. I've been there now. I prayed there. A woman wrote a song about recapturing it, the two-thousand-year wait, and the rededicating as ours again. And a girl was chosen to sing it. I know it in Hebrew. It's so moving. The melody is haunting, and the words more so. It's called 'Yerushalaim Shel Zaav' meaning 'Jerusalem of Gold.' "

I did my finger intro to the song on the guitar, and then began the Hebrew words. Gail, noticeably moved, sat down next to me on the bed as I played and sang, laying her hand on my thigh as she did so, as if to be one with me.

"I had forgotten how glorious your voice is, Jericho," Gail said after I finished singing. "How did I not give you the guitar when you first arrived? You could have sung me to sleep every night. And what a hauntingly beautiful song, just as you said."

I was glad for the song. It sealed us, somehow, even more than we were already.

But now I had to go back to Bern.

"Will I be melancholy today?" Gail mused aloud as she drove me to the train station. "I'll try to be grateful for having you back in my life again. And that I'll be seeing you whenever. Hopefully once every month or so."

"That's how I feel," I replied. "Until this weekend, you were out of my life. And now you're in it more than ever. I can only think of the future."

"Is there a future, love?"

"Nothing but."

She forced a smile onto her face and nodded slightly. "You must stay longer next time," she said as we walked toward the train to London that I was to catch.

"I know. But I'm still learning my job right now. I can't afford to take off more than a couple of days. I spent Friday night and Saturday getting to you: Bern to Basel, Basel to Paris—first class so I could unfold the seats into a bed and sleep a few hours—Paris to Calais, Calais to the white cliffs of Dover on hovercraft, Dover to London, London to here by Saturday afternoon. It's a haul, but I'll get to Bern by tomorrow."

"We can meet in London next time, if you like," she offered. "See the Queen, if you like. We never saw the Queen like we hoped."

"We'll talk. We're already talking. That's what keeps me going right now. You'll comfort me the whole train ride, just thinking of you."

"That's so bollocks, Jericho," she said with a laugh. "It's a dreadfully long train ride. You'll be bored and exhausted."

"What's bollocks? What does that mean?"

"The polite word is nonsense, I suppose," she explained. "You're just trying to keep a stiff upper lip. Which is good, but it's such a long journey. I do hope you think of me, but I'm not expecting it."

"But I love trains. And Texas is as big as France, so I'm used to traveling. I can handle it. And I'll be thinking of you, for sure. It'll preoccupy my emotions."

"You're such a dear. I suppose I must be optimistic too, then."

I leaned to kiss her.

"The train will be leaving soon," she said as she gave me a slight push from our embrace. "You better get on now. Then stick your head out the window so we can be star-crossed lovers like in the movies."

"I love England," I said before breaking loose from her. "Now even more. My girlfriend is British. I love that. I have a British girlfriend. That's special."

"Go on, you," she said with a laugh while pushing me away once more toward the train.

We searched the train cars until we found one only half full. I boarded it and quickly placed my backpack and guitar in the luggage rack over the seat where I would sit. Then I lowered the window to talk to Gail.

"This is really it, isn't it, love?" she said while raising her hand to touch mine as I stretched it out to her. "But no more wars to run off to. Or adventures. No more melodrama of heartaches. This time only fond farewells as lovers. At last. To think we had to be in our thirties before figuring out what we already knew."

"We took the scenic route getting here," I teased.

"Boy, did we ever."

The train suddenly made a small jerk, and the wheels squeaked on the tracks as they began to move.

"I'll walk beside you, and we'll clutch hands, pretending we're in love," she said, grinning. "Is this what we've dreamed of all our lives? We're doing it, love, romantic drama in abundance."

My smile broadened as my reply, while the train picked up a little speed.

"I love you, Jericho," she said, exuding emotion.

"I love you, Gail."

"I love you, Jericho. I really love you."

My mind scrambled. I couldn't stand goodbyes. I needed more than hope. I needed plans to see her again. Solid ones.

"Gail, listen. You're on the dole. I've got a job. Arrange somehow to come stay with me. Not just stay, but for a purpose. To work this out between us faster. Somehow we've got to get married eventually. Once we know we're for real."

"Just like that?"

"I want you in my life."

"Do you always get what you want?" she asked with a laugh.

"Yes," I answered.

"As long as I'm what you want, I'll arrange to come to Switzerland. I can manage a few days now and then. Do you think we'll make it? What if we aren't up to marriage? What if we fail in our courtship?"

"We've known each other for eight years," I mocked.

"But over half the time was figuring it all out," she replied.

"But now we have, Gail. I've known forever that I

wanted you. I never got over you. More than all those girls that threw themselves at me but somehow were never you. And all your men that you turned away, the Mr. Notrights. And you nearly died, indirectly from my inspiration, in the Himalayas. What other reason to not wait anymore after all that? We've paid our dues. Now comes the courtship in earnest."

The train picked up more speed, and we were forced to let go of our grip with each other. Gail began a jog to keep up.

"Goodbye, love," she said. "We'll talk about this."

"Talk, hell," I answered boldly.

"If we worked out, I'd have to give up my life on the dole," she said with a laugh.

"We'll live on love," I joked in return. "You'll love Switzerland. If any place is more beautiful than the Lakes, it's Switzerland. Beautiful in a different way, though. Majestic, in your face, bombastic beauty. The Lakes were tranquil, idyllic. The Alps are the same but different."

"Goodbye, my love," she said while blowing kisses at me. "Goodbye, darling. I'll do it. I'll come stay with you. We'll have a courtship. We'll be happy. But how will I work there if we do make it and get married? I don't speak German."

The train picked up more speed—enough, finally, that Gail had to stop running from the futility of it.

"Neither do I," I yelled in reply as she began to fade into the distance. "You can teach in a Montessori school or something. Or keep getting pregnant, perhaps, and raise our kids. Whatever suits you." I began to wave frantically. "I love you, Gail. I love you, Gail!"

I watched her diminishing figure until I couldn't

see her anymore. Then I closed the window and plopped down in my seat to savor the glory.

"I love you, Gail," I whispered to myself one last time. "I'm going to marry you someday. Someday soon."

A word from the author...

Born on October 7, 1948, in Harlingen, Texas, where I grew up and worked on a cotton farm, I graduated from Harlingen High School in 1966 and attended Texas A&M beginning in the summer of 1966. In January 1970 I dropped out to enlist in the United States Marine Corps, where I served as an enlisted man, attaining the rank of sergeant, with an honorable discharge after three years. I worked as a computer programmer afterwards in Houston and as a civil servant for a US Air Force Base in Frankfurt, Germany. I traveled and worked in Europe for two years, which included flying to Israel in October 1973 to aid the Jewish State in the Yom Kippur War. I was also in Greece in the summer of 1974 when the war between Greece and Turkey erupted over Cyprus. I was stuck on the Greek island of Ios for part of that war, until I managed to catch a boat to Athens just in time to watch the Greek military dictatorship fold. I returned to Texas A&M in the fall of 1976 to finish my bachelor's degree in Business Management. I returned to Europe afterwards and also to Israel, where I lived for almost a year. I later taught English in Taiwan before returning home in 1980 to get a master's degree in Agricultural Economics, received in 1982. I joined the US Peace Corps in 1984 and served for three years in the Philippines. In 1987 I began work for the Swiss government as a computer programmer until 1998. I have worked in the IT department of Texas A&M since 1998. I have three children and am presently divorced. I am Jewish.